Also by Sandi Layne

Éire's Captive Moon (Éire's Viking Trilogy Book 1)

*For Ruby ~
I hope you enjoy this story. God's best to you.*

An Unexpected Woman

By
Sandi Layne

Sandi Layne

The Writer's Coffee Shop
Publishing House

First published by The Writer's Coffee Shop, 2013

Copyright © Sandi Layne, 2013

The right of Sandi Layne to be identified as the author of this work has been asserted by her under the *Copyright Amendment (Moral Rights) Act 2000*

This work is copyrighted. All rights are reserved. Apart from any use as permitted under the Copyright Act 1968, no part may be reproduced, copied, scanned, stored in a retrieval system, recorded or transmitted, in any form or by any means, without the prior written permission of the publisher.

This book is a work of fiction. Names, characters, places and incidents are either a product of the author's imagination or are used fictitiously. Any resemblance to actual people living or dead, events or locales is entirely coincidental.

The Writer's Coffee Shop
(Australia)   PO Box 447 Cherrybrook NSW 2126
(USA)   PO Box 2116 Waxahachie TX 75168

Paperback ISBN- 978-1-61213-159-7
E-book ISBN- 978-1-61213-160-3

A CIP catalogue record for this book is available from the US Congress Library.

Cover image licensed by: © Depositphotos.com/photography33 and © Depositphotos.com/Yuri Arcurs
Cover design by: Megan Dooley

www.thewriterscoffeeshop.com/slayne

About the Author

Having been a voracious reader all her life, Sandi never expected to want to write until the idea was presented in a backhanded manner. Once the notion occurred to her, though, she had to dive in the deep end (as is her wont) and began by writing historical fiction. She has since written more than twenty novels—most of which will never see the light of day.

Sandi has degrees in English and Ministry, has studied theology, spent years as an educator, has worked in escrow and sundry other careers, but research is her passion. She won an award for Celtic Fiction in 2003, but as well as history, she is also fascinated with contemporary research and has self-published several novels in the Inspirational Romance genre.

She has been married for twenty years to a man tolerant enough to let her go giddy when she discovers new words in Old Norse. Her two sons find her amusing and have enjoyed listening to her read aloud—especially when she uses funny voices. A woman of deep faith, she still finds a great deal to laugh at in the small moments of the everyday and hopes that she can help others find these moments, too.

Author's Notes

For the creation of this unexpected woman, I thank my husband, Joe. He has given me endless information, answered a hundred questions, checked my details and—most importantly—smiled at the right places when he read the manuscript.

I also want to thank Wendy Perrotte and Alice Dyer for their eyes and minds. And my mother-in-law, Ruth Reis, who has always been willing to share her professional knowledge with me when I need it for my work. Thank you to Erin Morgan, Kathie Spitz, and Christine McPherson for their editing and polishing mojo. Finally, I want to send a thank you to Kevin McGrew, formerly of Vancouver, for his willingness to be included in a cameo.

To my Lord and God, I also give thanks. Thanks for an imagination that runs at all hours, for inspiration that surrounds me, and for the joys in the small moments of life. Truly, I am blessed beyond all deserving.

Sandi Layne

One

"In life, the ability to laugh is vital."

"Hello!" Mark Countryman called as he pushed open the glass door to the small Chinese take-out restaurant, China Town. "Just me."

"Hi, Mark," Anne, the woman behind the counter called back. "Taking this home today? Working hard?"

"Back to the office," he told her with a grin. "It's Wednesday."

"Ah, of course," the busy, slender woman said with a nod. They had become acquainted over the last several months. Anne was not, he was sure, her birth name, but she and the other people in the restaurant had evidently tried to do their best to make things easier on their patrons. He had discovered that Anne had three children, ranging in age from seventeen to five, which was surprising as she only looked to be about twenty-five herself.

She was, in fact, much closer to his own age of thirty-nine.

He gave her his order—surprising her when he ordered a different lunch combo than his usual. The phone rang behind the counter and Mark nodded, smiled, and sat in a sturdy metal chair. He didn't patronize this place because of the decor, he came for the food.

"China Town. Take out, okay. White rice? Okay. Phone number? Okay. About ten minutes. Bye."

While he waited, Mark watched the folks walking up and down the strip mall. He had been here for two years, coming through two mild hurricane seasons, but was still unused to the sight of people in shorts and T-shirts in the first weeks of March. In Glencoe, the small Californian mountain community that had been his home for many years, March was still winter, in both temperature and wardrobe. Snow still lingered in places, sweaters and jeans were everywhere. In Ohio, where he had been working until being called to his present church, winters had been even longer. But here in Southwest Florida, in the spread-out community of North Fort Myers, it was a time of shorts, T-shirts and flip-flops.

Shop doors were opened along the strip mall's cement walk and the breeze brought a distant taste of salt from the Gulf of Mexico to the discerning nose. The Caloosahatchee was only one air mile from this plate glass door. A large river, with tides and weekend regattas, it was also the backyard for many of the area's more well-to-do residents.

"Mark," Anne said, her voice echoing off the white walls as she lifted the white plastic bag with his lunch. "Ready!"

He paid for it, left her a tip, and was backing up to the door, telling Anne to have a good day, when the door opened and he collided with an incoming customer. "Whoa!" he exclaimed, arms flailing enough that he was relieved that all the food was secure inside well-packed containers.

"Hey!" the incoming customer said in response, her laughter warm as she caught him with one hand on either side of his ribs. "Steady, there," she advised, holding him until both his feet were firm on the faded tile floor. "Y'all right?"

"Yeah," he said, feeling more than a little embarrassed to have been caught so off-center, and to have been held up by a woman. Meeting her eyes, he had to catch his breath. "Thank you."

Her dancing brown eyes were bold below marked brown brows as she appeared to study him to assure herself he was, indeed, able to stand on his own. He had the definite feeling, though, that she was checking him out, which was disconcerting . . . and a little flattering. As brief as the contact had been, he felt the emptiness where her hands had braced him. Blowing out a puff of air, he tried to shrug the expectant feeling away.

Hands dropping to her sides, she nodded. "You're welcome. But hey, if you ever feel the need to step into a gravity well again," she said with a laugh, "I'll be more than happy to help." Her wink was playful and he knew that she could indeed be flirtatious, given the opportunity.

It was not in his nature, though, to provide one. He could only look at her in surprise and regret that he couldn't seem to respond in kind. He wanted to, but felt out of his depth with her. *And* gravity well? *Was that a new slang term or something?*

"Shelley, you're early," Anne said from behind the counter. "Busy day today?"

A strange upsurge of hope sent his eyebrows up. Shelley. Her name was Shelley and she was another regular at China Town. He knew he hadn't seen her here before.

"Oh, yeah. I've got such a route, today."

Her voice brought him back to the present, reminding him of his chagrin at having fallen right into this young woman's arms. He didn't stick around to eavesdrop on the conversation. He just wanted to take his disconcerted self out of China Town and back to the office, where things made more sense.

Except that they didn't make sense when he reached the church. A huge delivery truck from one of the local, upscale furniture stores was parked at the entrance, and there was a team of muscular fellows hefting a desk through the glass doors as Mark approached. This was a large church, as such concepts were reckoned. Not a mega-church, but large. He was one of three Associate Pastors on staff, with his primary area of responsibility being the Education Ministries. Although it was not as physically involving as Youth Ministry, he felt he might be getting too old for that himself. Oh, he knew of several youth pastors who were his age and older, but these days he was just as happy to be working in a less high-energy position.

Does that make me a wimp? he wondered with a grin. *Or just an old fogey?*

An image of the blond-haired, brown-eyed woman from the Chinese restaurant made him think that maybe he was. He had, after all, found the first few gray hairs at his temples just last week.

"Dr. Countryman," Letty said with a smile. She was the secretary he "shared" with the music minister. "Here are some messages for you, and don't forget to check your e-mail."

"What's with the delivery truck?"

Letty rose and gave him an invoice. "New furniture."

"I saw that," he remarked. "When did this happen?"

"Oh. They called on Monday, and Trish was at the front desk. They told her they'd be coming today to deliver all of this, but she, ah—" Letty shrugged with silent apology.

"Forgot? Yeah. So what're they doing?"

"Look at the invoice," Letty said, her voice more enthusiastic as she began discussing decorating. Her short, black hair fluttered around her head as she turned this way and that, watching as a desk was removed from one of the offices.

"Hey, that's mine!" Mark protested. "Wait a sec."

Letty put one well-manicured hand on his arm. "Hang on. I got your desk cleared off, with Pastor and Marianne helping. We were all taken by surprise, Mark."

He knew that Pastor Benjamin Keller and Marianne, Ben's secretary, would have done a fine job making sure his stuff was out of the way, but still, Mark was irritated at the unannounced change. He didn't want to express that to Letty, though, so he shook his head. "Okay. So how'd this happen?"

"See the invoice? Jacob Cairns apparently decided to surprise you guys and buy you all new office furniture. Look, in this collection there's a desk, bookshelves, and a file cabinet."

"What'd Pastor say?" he asked Letty, using the reference to their boss that the entire office used.

Letty slid a glance through slightly slanted eyes. "He was . . . surprised. Called Jacob to, um, thank him."

Her tone was rich in nuance. So was his. "Uh-huh. We'll have to make sure we all send him appropriate expressions of our gratitude." He grimaced as his bookshelves were carted down the hall, past the desk where he was standing with Letty, and down a short corridor to be deposited in the wide foyer of the building, where the church offices were housed under the same roof as the worship center.

Thanking Letty, Mark took advantage of the delivery men being out at the well-marked delivery truck to hurry to his office and see the chaos that was developing. His books were stacked against the far wall, under the windows, in rows about three books deep. With a sigh, he saw where his desk had been by the indentations on the carpet, and was thankful that no one had wheeled his chair out. He liked that chair and it was hard to find something truly comfortable. He had brought this one down from Ohio, and its brown leather ergonomic curves suited him well. Apparently, Mr. Cairns had not found it necessary to replace it.

He closed his eyes and remembered to give thanks for the generosity behind the gift of new office furniture. For every pastor on staff.

"Didn't have time to call and warn you, Mark, sorry." It was the senior pastor's resonant voice and Mark turned with a smile. Ben's expression was wry. "Mr. Cairns informed me that he will be coming out tomorrow to check the furniture to make sure it is in good condition."

"From this store? I'm sure it will be." The store was pretty much *the* premier furniture store in Florida. Mark had never even been in one of their showrooms. What was the point when he couldn't afford a lamp from that place, much less a sofa?

"Excuse us," one of the delivery men called, his voice sounding strained under the weight of a rather impressive desk. Ben had Mark chuckling by the dramatic way in which he drew himself up on the wall opposite where the desk would go. Between the two well-muscled delivery men, the desk made it through the door without mishap. "That's good," one of them, with the edge of a tattoo visible under the sleeve of his shirt, remarked. "Didn't have to take the legs off."

"Uh, yeah. Thanks. Good," Mark said when it appeared the man was waiting for a response.

"Be back with the bookcases next."

They left and Mark moved to the new desk strictly on autopilot. "Wow. Had you seen this before?" he inquired of his boss.

"No. It's good furniture, though."

"I didn't doubt that for a minute."

"Jacob wanted to give the church something practical, he said. Thought we could all use some new pieces." Ben knelt to examine the drawers and then the keyboard tray that slid out from under the main work surface of the desk. The dark wood gleamed in the overhead lighting. "He wanted it to be a surprise."

"Well, it certainly has been. Very generous of him."

"Mm." Ben didn't say any more than that and Mark let it go.

He moved to his next concern. "What about our old stuff? We've got everyone coming tonight and I'm guessing that the foyer will be full."

"Yeah," Ben said, pushing himself up to his full height of just under six feet. Mark himself was about six feet, so the two men were all but eye-to-eye. "Well. We'll just do the best we can. I'm thinking that Marianne, Letty, and Cris can sort through and recycle our old furniture. Might be able to donate some of it, too."

"Excuse us," The voice echoed down the hall, and the senior pastor and senior associate pastor hurried from that office down to one of the others, to be of what help they could.

"When I was in the Marines," Ben remarked with a laugh, "we had a motto."

"Semper Fi?" Mark guessed.

"No. Semper Gumby. Always flexible."

"Good motto."

"Here's my paperwork," Shelley Roberts told Dinah in Customer Service. "Where's my route for today?"

"And good morning to you," Dinah said, tucking a long section of chestnut-colored hair behind one ear. "Here you go. Parts are pulled. Some of 'em are over there at The Empty." The Empty was a customer service workstation that was uninhabited. It had been empty—ominously so, some might say—since the building was constructed. Management didn't want to hear anything about that, so it was a term only used by the furniture technicians and customer service representatives.

Shelley took the papers and nodded, her short blond hair scattering in playful disarray. She had the Naples route today. Most of her calls were down there anyway. Incredible houses. Luxury high-rises that just blew her mind on occasion. "Okay. I'll go get that stuff out to the van then."

"Wait!"

"What?"

Dinah shot her an incredulous expression. "Did you meet any cute ones yesterday?"

Shelley grinned. "Oh, yeah. One. Very hot. Very much a Tall, Dark, and Handsome."

Dinah sat back in her chair so that her pregnancy was obvious. "Oh? Isn't it just a shame that the TDH ones are customers?"

"Not this one. I saw him on lunch. Almost knocked me off my feet. Or," she amended with a twinkle in her eye, "maybe I knocked him off his."

"Tell!" Dinah demanded, busy hands beckoning for more information.

Shelley recounted her adventure, such as it was, of the prior afternoon.

"He was on his way out, though," she said with a dramatic sigh. "So I didn't get to find out his name."

"Too bad. But hey, there's always Bret . . ."

The young women erupted in giggles at the idea. Bret was a furniture technician, like Shelley, and had the reputation for hitting on every single female in the entire company. No matter their age or status, he gave it the old college try. It was sad, but it was also kind of funny. At least, Shelley thought so.

She checked The Empty for the parts that would be needed for the day and saw she would need something from the warehouse. Which was cool. She had worked there for years before being transferred permanently to doing the in-home service calls. With a bounce in her step, she entered the enormous building adjacent to—but completely different from—the main business offices of the company. "Hey!"

"Shell, good to see ya."

"Good morning!"

"How are ya?"

"Lookin' good."

"Your dad's over there."

The various calls, comments, and pointed fingers had her responding as she worked her way over to her dad's workstation. "Good to see you. Almost Friday. Hey, it's just the uniform, you know? Thanks."

The company's uniform for the service techs was extremely serviceable. A midnight blue polo shirt with the employee's name embroidered on the front in white and the company name and logo on the sleeve. It was paired with either slacks or shorts of an industrial-grade fabric, made to withstand hundreds of washings while maintaining the khaki color. Always worn with socks and hiking boots, sneakers, or steel-toed boots—depending upon what the individual tech decided was necessary. OSHA, probably, would prefer the steel toes.

"Shell, got your route for today?"

"Yeah, Dad. Just picking up some parts. How're you doing? How's Stephanie?" Her father's wife was technically her stepmother, but Shelley could not bring herself to call Stephanie anything but her name.

Dad had remarried only a few years back, so Stephanie didn't expect it either. Her father smiled a little and chucked her on the chin with a callused hand. "Doin' fine, hon. No worries. Steph's great. Got plans after church on Sunday?"

"Nope."

"Good. Come over for lunch."

"Who's cooking?"

"She is."

"Then I'll be there," Shelley assured her father.

After gathering her parts together and checking her map pages—she knew the Naples area, but it never hurt to double check—she climbed behind the wheel of her company service van and headed out for another day.

"Too bad I won't be in NoFo," she remarked to herself, referring to North Fort Myers, where she lived and, occasionally, worked. "Coulda been fun to see if Tall, Dark, and Handsome was eating Chinese take-out today."

As she did her service calls, Shelley always prayed for the customers she was sent out to help. Her job was part craftsman, part salesman, part fire-extinguisher. Throw in amateur psychologist, dog handler, lizard-wrangler, child-teaser, and encourager of some note, and she guessed that would go a fair way to describing her work. She prayed, though, for the people she saw. Prayed in a general way for their lives, prayed that she would do well for them, satisfying their concerns by one means or another at her disposal. She truly just wanted the best for them all. Even the ornery ones.

The following week, her resolve was tested again. It happened a couple times a month or so.

"Shelley, you get a fun one today," Dinah told her, moving a picture of her husband and pulling out the work orders for the day.

Taking the clipboard, Shelley flipped through the pages. "Which one? I don't recognize any of these addresses."

"The one at the church with the delivery damage. Mr. Cairns requested you."

"Cairns?" She drew a blank. "Not a clue."

"New stuff," Dinah pointed out, standing and rubbing at the small of her back. "See? Not his house at all. Look, it's a *church*."

The women grimaced over Dinah's desk. "Lovely," Shelley muttered. "Another Wednesday shot to Mars."

"Ha! You wish. And I thought you went to church?"

"I do. Not that one, but I do go. Cairns." She shook her head. "Well, if he asked for me, I guess I'll recognize him when I see him. And hey!" She grinned with a sudden thought. "Maybe Tall, Dark, and Handsome is at the Chinese take-out again."

"Super Shell to the rescue? He should *be* so lucky. You look like a superhero."

Shelley snorted. "Me?"

"Yeah, you're so athletic. And you have those great calf muscles, and some serious definition with your arms. Haven't seen your abs, but—"

By this time, Shelley was laughing silently into her paperwork. "I'm so *not* athletic. That's my brother's job. I just . . ."

"You just move furniture," Dinah whispered loudly. "We won't tell."

After collecting her parts for the day and checking in with her dad, as was her usual routine, Shelley was out into the breezy March morning. All during her first three calls, she was planning out a lunch hour stop at China Town. Maybe he'd be there. Same day of the week and everything.

Maybe. She wouldn't get to find out, though, until after that church call. So it was with a degree of impatience that she pulled up right in front of the main entrance, the company logo telling anyone who wondered who was imposing on their sheltered drop-off space.

Slipping her cell phone into a pocket on her shorts, her camera strap around one wrist and her clipboard in hand, she went through the doors, wondering what kind of delivery damage there might be and if she had any chance of being done in time to find Tall, Dark, and Handsome at China Town.

She had just come through the door when she was met by a face she definitely remembered. He had once left about two dozen tiny blue sticky notes on a coffee table. The table was distressed, meaning it was supposed to have the gouges and such in its surface, and was on the sales floor in that state—its proper state. Yet the man now facing her had gone round and round with her about it.

Dear Father in Heaven, she began silently as she came to him to shake his hand. *Please bless Mr. Cairns and his day. Let his business go well and may his attitude be bright. And please, Lord God, hide the sticky notes. Thank you!*

Two

". . . do not forget the zing!"

He really hoped that the service guy would arrive soon. Mark felt he had been fairly good-humored about having his office virtually upended for a full week, but he was getting a bit tired of having to sift through stacks of papers and books for studies and notes for his research and classes. Additionally, he would be preaching Sunday night, and this upheaval was not conducive to clear thinking.

He had given serious consideration to just working from home this week. "Maybe I should've," he remarked quietly to his computer screen as he played out the PowerPoint presentation for his evening class. Lights flickered on the phone. The intercom indicator. *Ah, maybe he's here, now. And I can get my books back up and my stuff organized again.*

It was unsettling, working like this. Mark really was unhappy that he was feeling so ungrateful, though. Jacob Cairns had done a generous thing—all right, maybe for a tax write-off, but still—and Mark told himself that he had to pray for an attitude adjustment.

"Ah, here you are. Pastor Keller, this is the, ah, furniture technician I *personally* requested to see to these repairs."

Ben's voice was low-pitched and neutral, Jacob Cairns's more strident. "Now, what happened," Mr. Cairns was saying as the group passed Mark's closed office door, "is that the delivery team was in a hurry. That's patently obvious. You'll just have to touch up what they messed up."

Then the voices were out of his earshot and Mark could only imagine they were going to Ben's office first. The senior pastor had been given not only a large desk, but also a bookcase that measured the length of one full wall, a pair of leather conference chairs and small occasional table, in addition to a pair of file cabinets in the same rich wood from which the rest of the furniture was crafted. The only thing he had seen wrong was that the desk wobbled. But Mark figured that was due as much to the floor of the office as it was to any "delivery damage" that Jacob Cairns was insisting be fixed.

Mark powered down his computer and left his Bible open—God's word was never wasted—on his new desk, and did what he could to tidy up the books he had been using. Wouldn't do to present a careless image to anyone. Soon enough, he heard Mr. Cairns escorting the service guy down the hall.

"Now, this is Dr. Countryman's office. I was really unhappy at the way the bookcases are standing. Not leveled at all. And there are several scratches on the desktop."

Surprised, Mark leaned over to examine the desktop. He didn't notice any scratches. He thought it looked to be excellent in quality and craftsmanship. The knocking on his door had him straightening his tie and forgoing his examination.

"Hello?"

"Dr. Countryman? May we come in?" Jacob Cairns's voice was now smooth, in the manner of a diplomat.

"Yes, please, I've been expecting you."

Then the door opened and Mark's jaw dropped. It was the young woman with the sure hands from China Town. "Well, I sure wasn't expecting *you*," he murmured directly to her.

Mr. Tall, Dark, and Handsome!

Shelley sent a quick *thank you* to the Lord for the opportunity just to see the man again. He had a name: *Dr. Countryman.* She tried to recover and remember everything her father had ever taught her about "appropriate behavior" toward a client when he first started taking her on calls. "Dr. Countryman, good morning. I, ah, wasn't expecting you either," she said with her best professional smile.

"You know him?" the customer, Mr. Cairns, inquired with some surprise.

Shelley couldn't seem to take her eyes from Dr. Countryman, but she did answer. "Not exactly, sir. We bumped into each other last week, but were not introduced." To the tallish man with the olive complexion, incredible dark eyes and still-incredulous smile, she extended her hand. "Shelley Roberts, Dr. Countryman. Let me take a look at your desk, all right?"

He shook her hand and Shelley had to look away and swallow hard to get her thundering heart back where it belonged. *Whoa.* She could not maintain eye contact. Compelling her expression to obedience, she found Dr. Countryman's face and noticed the interest in his eyes. That was encouraging.

She stepped past him to the desk, since Customer Cairns seemed to be very annoyed at its condition. "Ah, yes. Okay. There are some scratches to the finish here, and here," she remarked, hoping she didn't sound like some breathless teenager. "I can make those disappear."

"The drawers," Mr. Cairns said next. "They were making a strange sound when they closed. Dr. Countryman? Did you notice that?"

The question practically demanded that the office's main inhabitant answer in the affirmative. Shelley met Dr. Countryman's eyes as he said, "Maybe a slight banging sound, when they get fully closed."

"May I?" Shelley asked, moving around the desk, where his Bible was open. She smiled a little. "Romans. My dad always says that that book is like the How-to Book for Christians," she remarked as she knelt near the knee-hole of the desk and rolled open the lowest drawer. "Not peeking," she said, looking way up at Dr. Countryman and Mr. Cairns with what she knew was a reassuring manner. "Just listening to the glides." She heard the gratifyingly smooth sound of the drawer sliding out before she checked its balance and alignment. "Sounds good."

"But when it closes," Mr. Cairns reminded her, sounding insistent. "It has a hard sound."

Politely, she nodded and slid the drawer shut. It did have a bit of a metallic edge to it. "I can fix it so there's a bumper back there, sir." After checking the other desk drawers, she took pictures of the desktop. "Macro setting," she said, letting the men know what she was doing. "This will be on the file, so I can remember to have the right stains when I come back."

"When you come *back*?"

Both men had said that on the same breath. Shelley kept her expression politely neutral as she turned to face them fully. It was a little difficult. She felt almost as if Mr. Tall, Dark—*Dr. Countryman*—had sucked all the air out of the room with his sheer presence. She wasn't stupid. She knew it was entirely a chemistry thing, but it was still a little overwhelming for her. Still, she did her best not to heed it. "Yes, Mr. Cairns. Dr. Countryman. The work order only indicated there was delivery damage. There was no indication of how many pieces would need touching up. I don't have the time scheduled today to get all of this done. I'll have to reschedule and come out for probably a full day, if the other two offices are like the ones I have already seen."

"Seriously?" Dr. Countryman blurted out, sounding disconcerted. "I was really," he continued, smoothing his voice out a little, she noted, "looking forward to being able to get my books back on some shelves." He smiled disarmingly as he said this and she couldn't help but smile back. He had that kind of charisma.

Nodding, she said she understood. "Let me take a look at them," she offered.

Mr. Cairns accompanied her, pointing out a ding in the corner of one of the tall bookcases. "And here, too. Look at the scratches the delivery team made when they were putting the shelves in."

Shelley nodded, wishing Mr. Cairns would back off and give her a little room. He smelled like her last not-quite-boyfriend. Gucci aftershave that was a little too expensive. Not her favorite, for more than one reason. "Let me take some pics of this, too," she said, swinging her camera up. After doing so, she glanced back at Dr. Countryman who was leaning resignedly against his brand new desk and eyeing his books. "Look. Let me go get the pictures of the other pieces. Then I'll come back and try to get these level for you, okay?"

"Really?" he asked, his head seeming to jerk in surprise.

She grinned at him. "Yes. But," she went on, putting her grin away in favor of a "laying down the law" face for a customer, "if you want these scratches and that ding fixed when I come back, you'll need to have your books off those shelves. This one here and that one and the one down below on the other case. All right?" She really did not like moving a customer's personal possessions, whether it was books or porcelain sculptures out of a curio cabinet.

His answering smile was warm. "All right."

She wanted to sigh—maybe even swoon—but nodded instead and left the office on Mr. Cairn's heels. While taking pictures of another desk with delivery scratches, a chair with wobbly wheels, and more dings on more bookcases, Shelley said all the right things to the new owners of the furniture Mr. Cairns had purchased. Then, she made a few notes on her paperwork and tried to return to the van.

"Now just a moment, young woman," Customer Cairns said, coming to stand in front of her.

She couldn't just walk around him. No, at all times she had to be respectful. In her line of work the customer was not always right, but they did require a good hearing and some definite pacification. "Yes, sir?"

"I paid good money for these pieces," he said, his voice low and intense, as if to try to intimidate her. "I want them taken care of immediately."

She made sure she was at her reassuring best. "I understand, sir. I want to give each of these pieces the time they deserve. But I can't do that today, with my current route. To do it properly, I'll require at least four hours, I'm thinking. Maybe more. I'll want to dedicate half a day to these pieces exclusively, to do the job right, and I can't do that today." She smiled a little disarmingly. "The work order wasn't very specific, as I said earlier. The office didn't know to allow time for so many pieces."

He looked disgruntled. "Well, I can't be here for another day."

"I've got pictures of everything you pointed out, Mr. Cairns. I'll make sure to take care of each thing. Shall I ask Customer Service to call you for the rescheduling, or should they call the church's office?"

"Here. Have 'em call here. I can't make it. But I will," he added with a warning frown, "be in touch with Pastor Keller about it."

"I'm sure you will. Now, if you'll excuse me, sir, I have to get the tools to level the bookcases in Dr. Countryman's office."

This is just nuts.

Mark fidgeted at his desk, trying to add notes for his lesson that night, but all he could do was remember the last time a woman had knocked the breath out of him like Shelley Roberts had.

Her name was Dawn. A beautiful single mother with blond hair and blue eyes, she had been raising a teenage daughter all on her own. Her ex-boyfriend, Garrison, had been, and still was, a friend of Mark's. Knowing himself attracted to the mother of his friend's daughter, Mark had actually checked with Garrison before asking Dawn out. He remembered exactly when he knew he had fallen in love with her—it hadn't taken him long at all. That feeling, the surety of it, had been a quiet strength in him.

It just hadn't been a *mutual* feeling. Though Garrison had wronged Dawn in the worst possible way when they had both still been in high school, she had grown to care for him when they met again. Their relationship had grown around their daughter, PJ—a girl in Mark's youth group, now in her twenties—and it had been a beautiful example of forgiveness.

Mark had bowed out, Dawn and Garrison had married, and Mark moved across the country. God's hand had been obvious in that relationship. Today, Mark was pleased to call Garrison and Dawn Chase his friends. It had been a long time ago. He had never felt like that for anyone else, though. Not in all the years since. Sometimes, out of sheer loneliness, it was easy to want to try to *make* a relationship work. *That* hadn't worked well for Mark either.

Thankfully, he and Christina in Ohio had come to the mutual realization that wishing did not make it so; not even for two committed Christians who were trying hard. Too hard. His relationship with her had ended in much the same way as his time with Dawn—losing out to an old flame. He'd been pleased for Dawn and happy for Christina, but he missed the companionship.

He didn't want to go through all that again. Closing his eyes, Mark wasn't sure what to do. She was *there*. Occupying far too much mental space for someone he had met only a couple of times. It was like being a teenager again. Like he had no kind of control of his thoughts around her.

Lord, he prayed, as he had many times before, *I don't want anyone unless you want her for me. So, please, put a bow around her, like that song I heard over the holidays said, would you? So I know? I want only what you want for me. I don't want to blow it again.*

Less internally agitated, he was able to greet Shelley the furniture technician in a more settled manner. "I really appreciate this," he told her when she returned, small black bag in one hand.

"Not a problem. Now, if you'll just step back," she advised him, indicating the area behind his desk with a look, "I'll just get these bookcases level for you."

She knelt to check something before grimacing and rising to run her hand along the back of the bookshelf. When he saw her hand again, she was holding a red plastic bag. Without discussion, she opened it, checked the contents, and sighed.

It was pretty quiet which made him a little uncomfortable. "You mentioned that your dad said something about the Book of Romans?"

"Yep," she said, tossing him a quick smile over her shoulder before twisting her body almost impossibly around to snag the tool bag. "It can't be an original," she added before sliding out a small bar that Mark recognized to be a flat-headed screwdriver.

"It's not. So, ah, do you go to church?" he asked next. It was a nonthreatening question. She was, after all, *in* a church. He was no stranger to sharing his faith, but it was best to walk carefully in a professional relationship.

"I do," she told him. "Not this denomination," she clarified with another glance that seemed to twinkle even in the indifferent indoor lighting. "The Bible is still the Bible, though, isn't it? Now, I am going to have to lay this down, so make sure to stay where you are, all right, sir?"

He hadn't fully grasped what she said until she was in the middle of doing it: tilting the heavy bookcase and bringing it gently down to rest on its side on the floor. He had shifted that unit a bit himself last week, and knew how heavy it was. Embarrassed, he tried to apologize for not offering to help.

She laughed lightly. "This is my job, Dr. Countryman. I do it all the time. That one in the bigger office would be a two-man job, though, if it needed leveling. That's what these things are, by the way. Levelers."

"Does it?" he asked, because he enjoyed her voice. A vivid voice in a medium range that made him think of cheerleaders and being a youth pastor again.

"Need leveling? No." She attached four long levelers to the four corners of the bookcase. "There we go."

"Let me help you get it back up," Mark offered, stepping around the desk.

She only tossed him her smile again, the same one that she had offered him at the Chinese take-out place. "Not necessary, honest. Besides, you're not dressed," she said, squatting to grasp the top of the bookshelf, "for hefting furniture. Trust me."

Nonplussed, he could only watch as she stood slowly up and, with careful placement of her hands, maneuvered the bookshelf back to where it had been. He watched as she used the screwdriver-looking tool to make some adjustments in practically invisible holes before putting some small brown circle things in them. Then, she tried to rock it, but it didn't budge. "Wow. That was pretty complicated," he remarked.

"Not bad at all." Then, with a lifted brow, she added, "No Gravity Wells!"

So she remembered. Gratified, he grinned. "So you meant that to be about my, ah, near miss last week?"

"That's what I blame it on, anyway. You know, when I trip or something. Dense gravity." In a swing of her body, she moved up her tool bag again. "Hey, any excuse is a good one."

He eyed her carefully. She was a little above average in height, he guessed. Sturdy-looking. Not big, just sturdy. Athletic. "Were you on a softball team or something in college?" She blinked and laughed before proceeding to the next bookcase. This time he didn't offer to help at all. It was, he admitted to himself, a pleasure to watch her work. He had to remind himself not to stare.

"Me? No, sir. Didn't go to college and I didn't have time for sports in high school. My brother is the athlete. I worked with my dad." Mark was really impressed that she was able to continue the discussion while lowering the bookcase to the floor and installing the levelers. "What about you?"

"Me?"

Her blush was unexpected, covering most of her face and slipping down her throat. "Sorry, sir. I didn't mean to pry. Look, just about done here."

Wanting to put her at her ease again, he cast about urgently for another topic. Not only for her, but for himself. He didn't want to leave an impression of any sort of indiscretion on her part to color her memory. "Not prying at all. You're only establishing a basis for mutual understanding," he ventured. "And no, I wasn't much into sports in high school or college." He laughed lightly. "I guess I was kind of a geek."

"You?"

"Me."

Up went the second bookcase and in went the screwdriver. "There you are, sir. I hope you can get your books back up in short order. I'm not sure when they'll reschedule you—um, this call—but I'll try to make sure I am the one who comes out. I'm usually in North Fort Myers on Wednesdays."

"So you have a regular route for this kind of thing?" He was honestly curious.

She offered him half a shrug. "Generally. We'll get it taken care of, though. One way or another."

"I'm sure you will, Miss Roberts."

For just a second, he wanted to find something else to say to her. There was a sense of expectation about her, too, and that was intriguing. Her lips parted, in fact, but neither of them had words to fill a silence that suddenly became charged.

She recovered first. Casting her gaze to her arm, she made a show of checking her watch. "Well, sir. I'll be back."

"Good." He had just one more question. "May I ask you something before you go?"

"Sure."

"What's your favorite book of the Bible?"

She had not been expecting that, he could read in the lifting of those dark brown brows and widening of the lively eyes. She didn't hesitate to answer. "James. Now there's a writer who was very *in your face*, you know? I like that. See you next time, Dr. Countryman."

"I hope so," he murmured as she left his office. The book of James. He was completely, unexpectedly, *unsurprised*.

Three

"You haven't the faintest notion of getting married."

"So, any cute ones yesterday?" Dinah asked over a cup of tea. Not coffee, as Shelley had learned. Herbal tea. Something good for expectant mothers.

Shelley's smile was a little rueful. "Yeah. Definitely a TDH."

"Another one? Wow, you get all the luck." Dinah stretched her torso a little, her wince clear in the corporate fluorescent lighting.

"Not another one, no. The *same* one."

"Where? Which one?" Then Dinah's face fell. "Wait, that means he's a customer, right? That stinks."

Shelley paused while flipping through her call sheets for the day. "Is he, though? I mean," she clarified without a blush, "it's not like *he* bought the furniture. Even the church didn't buy it. Mr. Cairns did."

The mild aroma of chamomile wafted up as Dinah set her cup down carefully. "Yeah, but he's the one you're working for. Or with. Or whatever. He's the one there, so I think that'd qualify."

Shelley winked. "I won't be working there forever."

"Ha! Let's hope not."

Thursday and Friday were good days. Most of her calls were complete, meaning that she fulfilled the repairs to the customer's satisfaction. Sometimes it was as simple as dropping off new cushions for a sofa, other times it was as difficult as repairing grout and then buffing out the stone top of some patio furniture. Shelley had even had cause to drive past the church where Mr. Tall, Dark—*Dr. Countryman*—worked. Whenever she did, she slowed down a little. Just wondering if she might see him.

"Okay, so who is it?" her dad asked her Saturday morning. He had come over with Stephanie to help paint her kitchen. Stephanie was a genius with stencils.

"Yeah," Stephanie said, her voice teasing as she balanced on the Formica countertop. "I keep checking with your dad to see if it's one of the guys in the warehouse."

Her father, on a ladder to paint around the fan on the ceiling, chuckled. "Hardly, Steph. I keep telling you."

A glob of "eggshell white" fell on the plastic sheeting near Shelley's feet. "What makes you think there's a *somebody*, you two?" She refused to take her eyes from the door frame, where she was brushing on a second coat of glossy, barn-red paint.

"I've seen you get preoccupied before, Shell," Dad reminded her, his voice a little strained as he arched awkwardly to reach a spot. "Same thing. Different guy. I hope."

"Yeah. Gucci-Man is *historical*."

"Good," Stephanie called, shifting as she moved to the next stencil segment. "He was—"

"I know." Shelley laughed with some self-deprecation. "I did figure it out eventually. No, there isn't anyone. Not really."

"Uh-huh," her father said, sounding more amused than anything. "So, where did you *not* meet this man?"

Capitulating, Shelley set the slender paintbrush into the small paint tray. "All right. I met him at China Town. He's very well educated *and* has a good, steady job."

On the counter, Stephanie chuckled. "And he's probably, oh, closer to my age than yours, right?"

Stephanie was fifty, with white-white hair and a virtually wrinkle-free face. Shelley thought she was lovely. She nodded. "You do know my taste in men. But really, I'm not sure how old he is."

"So what's the problem?" Stephanie asked, avid interest sparking in her wide eyes.

"He's a customer."

"Oh . . ." Steve and Stephanie Roberts stopped their work for a moment and looked at her in all seriousness.

"Yeah."

Her dad laughed. "Well, he won't be one forever."

"That's what I'm figuring," Shelley told them both. "I can be patient."

They were still calling her *Patience* when they saw her at church the next morning.

"Patience," her father began, with a far-too-cheerful grin on his face. "Linda Arlenson is looking for you."

"The Sunday School Director?" Trepidation took a quick walk through her middle. "Where is she and what'd she want?"

Stephanie shifted her Bible from one arm to the other. "She didn't say, but she did have a copy of something that looked like curriculum on her. She might be over near the preschool classes."

Shelley closed her eyes. "Great. If she thinks I can take on a group of four-year-olds at the last minute—"

"Shelley! There you are."

Turning away from the laughing looks from her dad and his wife, Shelley met the harried smile and bright green eyes of the Sunday School Director. *It's a volunteer position*, she reminded herself. *She's not a professional. She doesn't do this to bug you.* "Hey, Linda. I heard you were looking for me."

"And I found you! I'm so glad."

Shelley braced herself and ran a hand over her hair. "What can I do for you?"

Linda bit her lip and looked up at her a little. She was about three inches short of Shelley's own five-foot-nine. "Well. You did such a great job with the kids at Vacation Bible School last year that we were wondering if you'd be willing to teach this year?"

Uncertain, Shelley cocked her head. "Who's *we*?"

"The VBS Director and me, of course. He's putting a team together and wants you to be on it."

"Can I get back to you?"

"Of course. And," Linda went on, a slightly cajoling lift of her chin warning Shelley in advance, "would you be willing to sub this morning for the fourth through sixth grade girls?"

Now that that shoe had fallen, Shelley wasn't feeling so uncomfortable. "This morning?"

Linda looked disconcerted. "I know it's last minute, but there's that flu bug going around and our usual subs aren't able to be here either. I've got the lesson here ready to go. Copies of the worksheet and the craft materials are in the room, with the snacks."

Before Shelley knew where to look, she had the lesson in her hand and was standing in the door where the long tables were occupied by a variety of little girls. "Miss Shelley," one of them called, a big grin on her tanned face. "I remember you."

"Well, that's good," Linda said, smiling with relief as she backed out of the room. "I'm sure it'll be a good morning then."

With only a moment to look at the lesson, Shelley took a deep breath and sent up a quick prayer. *Please, Lord, let me do this well and not blow it.*

Then, to the girls in front of her, she offered a lopsided smile. "Hello! Before we get started, let's pray, okay?"

She had never received any real training to do this, unlike working with furniture or as she had when her mother had taught her how to crochet as a girl. Shelley liked the girls, but felt out of her element in terms of teaching them anything. Wished she didn't. She wished she knew someone she could ask about this stuff without looking like a complete dufus. So she prayed, more out of a sense of hidden desperation than anything, and went to the first item on the copied lesson.

It was a game. She did all right with games. She tried her best and could only hope that, somehow, the girls would hear something in this hodge-podge of a lesson that they could take home with them.

"Great lesson, Dr. Countryman."

"I haven't heard anyone teach on that passage in a while. Nice job."

"I really enjoyed the lesson, Pastor."

Mark took the compliments with a small smile, thanked God in his heart, and prayed that, maybe, something would still be with these people Monday morning as it seemed to be Sunday evening. Shaking hands, thanking people, nodding at Ben and smiling at Ben's wife. And of course Kristi, the Children's Director and her husband, who was also named Mark. Everyone was here this evening, as they were building up to Easter. Palm Sunday was next week. Mark would be preaching at the Sunrise Service for Easter, leaving Ben to preach for both the hugely attended services at the regular times.

Mark hadn't bothered with a tie or jacket for the evening service. He was comfortable in a dress shirt and slacks as he returned to his office with its brand new furniture. Just a glance at the bookshelves made him smile with the memory. *Shelley Roberts.* The young woman with the sure hands and engaging grin that made her so appealing, even if her youthful exuberance did make him feel just a little . . . old. It wasn't even that she was what they'd called a "Wow" where he grew up. She was healthy and vibrant, more than just *pretty*. He had read a book once, where the description used for one of the characters was that a man would have to be very much in love with her to think she was *beautiful*, but she was just so appealing that all the male eyes in the room were drawn to her. Shelley was rather like that. Her smile was too broad, her chin too square, really, to be what he would call *beautiful*. But it had been days now, and he could still see her kneeling in front of the bookcase, twisting that leveling tool so he could shelve his books again. And here he was, still smiling about it.

And still hoping that the next time someone came to fix the furniture, it would be *her* and that he might get to talk to her again. She had said that her favorite book of the Bible was James. *That would be a great place to start.*

Still smiling, he set his Bible on the new desk and settled in his old chair to check his e-mail before heading home. A note from his older brother, Matt. He was a banker in California. There were pictures from his sister, Joanna. His niece and nephew were growing all the time. They had just celebrated their birthdays—her eleventh and his eighth. Luke was off somewhere doing some kind of cable show as an art director, so they rarely heard from him. His family was very close. These connections had kept him grounded when his heart had needed healing. Mark thanked God for all of them, every day.

There was also an e-mail from Garrison Chase, in California.

> To: Mark Countryman
> From: Garrison Chase
>
> Mark,
>
> Hello! How's Florida treating you? We're gearing up here for spring, but there's still some snow on the ground. Bet you haven't seen any of that in a couple of years, eh? Spring break is coming and Dawn and I thought we'd like to see Florida, kind of like a second honeymoon. Peej will take care of her little brother, so that'll work out well. We'll be staying at this hotel [he included a link] and Dawn thought that might be near you. It'd be great to see you, if you've got some free time that week. I bet it's kind of crazy. So, if you've got some good tourist ideas, send them over. I think we still have your cell phone number if it's the same as it was last year. Dawn said to tell you she is always open to the idea of a double date, too. So if you're seeing anyone, we'd love to get together with the two of you.
>
> We'll call when we get settled in our hotel.
>
> Garrison

The e-mail brought both a smile and a small sigh to Mark as he read it for a second time. It had been years since he had seen Garrison and Dawn Chase. Yes, it would be good to see them. *What is Dawn up to with the double date idea, anyway?*

Is that even fair? he wondered. But then, he was of course "over" Dawn Packard Chase. And she had never really known how he had felt about her, so she was only being friendly, he knew. The fact that he had his head wrapped around a woman he had only barely met and whom he could instantly visualize making a double date happen with, was certainly not something Dawn knew anything about.

> To: Garrison Chase
> From: Mark Countryman
>
> Garrison,

> Good to hear from you. It's definitely spring here already. College kids are all over the place to celebrate spring break. You wouldn't believe how close your hotel is to my new place. Yes, my cell number is the same and it'd be great to get together. Believe it or not, I haven't done much of the tourist thing around here yet. I do know some locals, though, and I'll ask them what they think, or you might be able to ask one yourself. Give my best to Dawn, P.J. and Nick.
>
> Mark

After sending that, he pursed his lips and blew out a breath. Well. He was done here for the night. Undoubtedly, everyone else had already left. Sundays were times for family.

He was surprised to get an answer from Garrison so quickly. "Guy's gotta be sitting on top of his keyboard."

> To: Mark Countryman
> From: Garrison Chase
>
> Mark - Don't think I missed the reference to the possibility of your bringing someone. Nothing would make us happier, as I'm sure we've told you before. So, have you met someone?
>
> - G.

Privately, Mark thought that Garrison might have carried his own piece of baggage about Mark's love life. After all, Garrison did marry the woman that he knew Mark to be interested in. Not that any of them would wish it to be otherwise, as things now stood.

If he answered, he'd never hear the end of it. But Garrison knew of his history and would make a good sounding board if the situation warranted. And Garrison was not only in a successful relationship at present, but his first marriage, to Clarissa, had been exemplary, too. Didn't the Bible say to seek wise counsel?

"Fine," he muttered, standing up, but typing on his laptop.

> To: Garrison Chase
> From: Mark Countryman
> Garrison,
>
> Maybe? Don't know, to be honest. I have a mixed track record. I'll let you know.
>
> Mark

After locking up the church, Mark cruised by China Town, part of him wondering if he might see *her* there. Anne kept the place open until nine every night of the week, so it was easy enough for him to enter and order. But Anne wasn't behind the counter. It was a new girl. Someone he didn't know and, that evening, he just did *not* feel up to meeting anyone new. Ordering a pint of beef fried rice to go, he contented himself with watching the foot traffic outside the plate glass windows.

Driving home was a quick trip. He saw the hotel where Garrison and Dawn would be staying. "It's a great view," he said aloud as he pulled into the lot where he lived, about fifty yards from the hotel.

The little condo community on the bank of the Caloosahatchee was extremely well-maintained, but the individual residences were very small. Still, the fresh black pavement, the real brick paving stones on the walks, and the thick green grass all looked fresh off a brochure. He lived in an end unit, right next to the river. It was a mere half dozen steps down the lawn from his door to the water's edge. Not even a rail to separate The Walk from the water.

It had been such a deal, too. It had been a buyer's market when he bought it.

He opened the door and smiled a little as he flipped the switch. The only downside to the deal had been that his new home had been out-of-date. So, slowly over the past two years he'd replaced the carpets, repainted the interior, and updated the cabinetry. Fortunately, members of the church had been willing to help out, so all he had had to do was supply the materials and rip the paneling from the walls. Now, he concluded as he slid off his shoes, he just wanted to pick up a few odds and ends to flesh things out. He wanted some items for his kitchen, too, so he would likely have to do some shopping soon. After all, he might be having guests when Dawn and Garrison came out, and they'd give him a hard time if it looked as if he were living in a generic rental instead of a riverfront condo.

Truth was, he had put off personalizing the place. He had hoped—prayed—that he would have found someone to share this cozy place by now. To share his life. To share his ministry, even. Hindsight being what it was, he could see that neither Dawn nor Christina would have been good partners in that regard.

Maybe, Lord, I'm not cut out for a life's partner? Am I supposed to be single? Is that what this is all about?

It hurt to even think that, and he leaned back heavily against the door of his home.

The following morning, after his devotionals and a quick breakfast, he went to a couple of stores across the river in Fort Myers. He wasn't sure exactly what he was looking for, but he didn't find it. Then he remembered the coupon mailer he had received from Costco and decided to go there. It was a good half hour's drive from his place, so he didn't shop there all that often. After all, he was just a single guy and buying in bulk seemed like overkill at times.

It felt almost like submission, shopping for decorative items. *Is that the answer then, Lord?* he wondered as he drove over the Caloosahatchee Bridge, the morning sun glinting off small waves below. *Is doing this accepting no one else will be doing it? That I'll be alone?*

He wasn't expecting an answer, and the vague sense of anticipation he felt in his midsection was not reassuring.

Pulling into the thronged parking lot, he found a spot next to a tiny yellow Mini Cooper convertible. He was kind of pleased about that, because such a small car left him plenty of room to get in and out of his own Toyota. Feeling more optimistic, he chose a shopping cart and wove between the other shoppers into the huge warehouse store. Many of these shoppers were retirees, he was fairly certain. White of hair and trendy of wardrobe, they were tanned and looked as if they had just come from the local country club.

Large televisions met him first in an entertainment component section. He didn't spend a lot of time watching television, though he did have a couple of shows he tried to catch when he could. He had an iPod, so a stereo wasn't high on his list of priorities either. Up the left side, he wove the aisles of the store, looking at some decorative items. He found, though, a new toaster oven. And there was a set of baskets, which would work for holding his magazines so he could get them off the coffee table. He put both items in his cart and proceeded past the center section, where there were books and DVDs, but nothing appealed to him just now.

He had just decided to take a quick pass by the dairy section to get a carton of eggs to make deviled eggs for lunches, when he stopped short before lurching forward a little with his shopping cart. A young woman was lifting a flat of bottled water from the concrete floor. His first instinct was to offer his assistance, but then he was struck by the way in which she moved and he realized he knew her. He couldn't seem to breathe for a moment.

"Miss Roberts?" he asked, pushing past that breathless issue. The smile she flashed him over her bare shoulder was *definitely* the one he remembered. "I almost didn't recognize you out of uniform," he said, flustered.

She turned, setting the flat of water into her own cart, seemingly without effort. "Oh, this?" she asked, holding out the long floral skirt of her halter-dress. "Believe it or not, I'm usually a very girly girl."

Still working around his appreciative surprise, Mark could only nod and try hard not to stare at her. At the expanse of bare skin on her upper back, the small pale oval on her shoulder blade that had grabbed his attention. Embarrassed and not wanting to give her any inappropriate impression, he pulled his attention back to her face with an effort.

"Do you normally go through a lot of bottled water while you work?" he asked in a bid to have something to say before she walked away. He didn't entirely understand himself, but there it was. *Oh, Lord,* he prayed silently. *I thought, I thought that—. Wasn't this about being single?*

A brisk shake of Shelley Roberts's head was followed by another smile. "Nope. I just start stocking up for hurricane season in March, see. Never know when the first storm might hit."

"Already?"

"Oh, yeah. I do a little bit with every paycheck," Shelley told him. "Water, batteries, replacements on any of my battery-operated gear. Gas for my generator, food, and this year I'm going to get new storm shutters. I've been saving for them. My plywood is getting warped."

Impressed, he could only nod. "Wow. You're really going to be prepared."

"What about you?" she asked, staring into his eyes. "When do you get started?"

He shook his head. "I haven't really done a whole lot of that."

"What? Are you kidding me?" Her mouth dropped open and she looked prepared to read him the riot act or something. The idea made him smile inwardly. "Have you *seen* Sanibel and Captiva since Cyrus came through a few years ago?"

"Um, no. I've never been there."

Incredulity sparked from her eyes. "Never?"

"Never."

Her mouth fell open again. "Dr. Countryman. How long have you lived here?"

He smiled a little, enjoying the enthusiasm she brought to the conversation. "This will be my third summer, but I've been here a little more than two years."

"Oh, *that* explains it."

"I actually haven't even seen the beach since I moved here," he told her, wanting to watch her react again. It was a rejuvenating experience.

She rolled up in her nearly nonexistent sandals. "What?" A laugh in her voice, she pointed to his cart and said, "Okay. Do you have anything perishable in there?"

"No . . ."

"Then check out. You're coming with me. We're going to the beach. It *is* your day off, right?"

Laughing in sheer shock, he nodded. "Yeah, but—"

"Not another word, Dr. Countryman. Come on. I cannot *believe* you've been here that long and haven't seen the beach."

He wanted to accept—wanted to accept with more strength than was comfortable—but he thought he better ask one question. "Just a second. Are you asking me out?"

Four

"We can talk about just about everything..."

A few colorful terms she had heard over the years flew through Shelley's mind, but she didn't give any of them voice. Was she asking him out? Mr. Tall, Dark, and Handsome? Oh, wouldn't she like to? *Yes.* But was she?

"Um, no," she said, blushing in her embarrassment. He was a customer so she could *not* ask him out, for one. For another, her mother had written, a long time ago, not to ask a guy out. *"Men like the pursuit,"* Mom had said. *"So let them chase!"* It was a rule she had taken to heart, since her mother had found it important enough to write about, and she had never really regretted it.

When she was able to look him in the eye again, she saw only a polite acceptance, as opposed to the amusement and interest he had been showing. *Chemistry,* she reminded herself. *Chemistry is all it is, girl.* She didn't want him to refuse to come with her, though. The invitation had been spur-of-the-moment, but she meant it. "So! Um, you're a minister at that church, right?"

His nod was slow, as if he was wondering what she was up to; she didn't blame him. "Yes. Is that a problem?"

She hastened to reassure him. "Not even. No. I just wondered what it was you, um, specialized in, you know? Like, are you the music minister or something?"

He laughed and leaned over his shopping cart. It was only then that she noticed the absolutely incredible dimple at the corner of his smile. It didn't always show up, but it was there now and she had to make herself look away from it.

"I'm the Education Minister, actually. I mean, that's what I oversee at the church. I also teach at the midweek Bible studies, and occasionally preach Sunday nights. Why?"

"Well, that's perfect," Shelley said, impressed. "See, I sometimes sub for Sunday School and stuff, and I worked some with VBS last year, and they've asked me to teach again this year."

He nodded. "And . . . what does that have to do with going to the beach?" he asked, looking as if he was going to decline and disappear.

She gave him her best smile. "Well. See this is what I was thinking. I need help. I've never been, you know, trained in how to teach, right? I mean, I learned my job from my dad, but no one ever taught me how to teach God's word. *You* know how. So how about if you help me? Then, see, we'd be bartering." She nodded. It made perfect sense to her. She really hoped it made sense to him, too. *I'm not asking him out, Mom,* she said silently. *I'm simply going for a fair trade, right?*

He appeared to consider it, the humor returning to his dark eyes, lips twitching against what had to be that knockout smile. "Bartering. All right," he said in concession while shoppers hurried past them. "On one condition."

"Name it," she blurted, thankful he was not turning her down entirely.

"My name's Mark, okay? Not Dr. Countryman. Not Pastor. Just *Mark*."

"Then I'm Shelley. Not Miss Roberts. Deal?"

"Deal."

She held out her hand to shake on it. A simple handshake seemed to draw the two of them into a cone of silence or something, though, and Shelley felt, suddenly, very self-conscious and very aware of Dr. Countryman—*Mark*—all at once. From his thick dark hair to the toes of his sneakers. *Patience*, she told herself, a laugh bubbling under the surface.

He appeared to study her hand for a moment before slowly letting it go. "How do you want to do this, then, Shelley?" he asked at last, breaking the silence and allowing her to breathe again.

She blew out a breath. *He said yes! Good. Wow. That was fast. How do we do this? I'm not worried about being with him; I'll be totally safe, I'm sure.* "Well. Let me get one more flat of water," she said, her heart pounding rather harder than normal, "and if you're ready, we can check out. I'll drive, so you can do the tourist thing." She was disconcerted, though, when he slid a flat of water from another stack of them. "You—um, you don't have to do that."

His grin was easy. "I know."

Blowing out a breath, she pulled her cart back and the two of them started toward the main traffic aisle on this side of Costco. She smiled a little at the people she maneuvered around, very mindful of Mark being behind her. She couldn't really make conversation over her shoulder or anything, because she didn't want to bump into anyone. But then, someone called out his name and she stopped, too.

"Dr. Countryman!"

Shelley pulled her cart out of the general walk. She didn't want to eavesdrop or intrude into his conversation with someone. Who knew?

Maybe it was someone from his church. He greeted the couple that had approached. Nice looking people. The lady had a Mercedes fob dangling on her handbag and the man was wearing Tommy Bahama gear. If you live in Southwest Florida, some forms of identification are automatic, and she saw that this was a couple who had some money and wanted others to know about it. Sometimes, Shelley ran into former customers when she was out and about. She tried very hard to make herself unobtrusive when that happened, for they often asked her to come out again, off the books, and there were rules about that, too. She tried not to stare at the "money markers", as she called them. It was rude.

Trying not to be obvious, she still kept an eye on Mark. He was intriguing. He had to be at least in his mid-thirties, she judged. And he was single? And a minister? There had to be a story there, and she was interested in finding out what it was. She heard plenty of stories out on the job. Many of her customers stayed with her while she worked on their expensive furniture—she didn't blame them, but it could get uncomfortable and boring—and they talked about many things. Politics, religion, child-rearing, hurricane season, books, television, their states of origin. She imagined that nothing Mark Countryman could ever say would be boring.

Yes, Shelley. You are smitten. Own it.

Mark flickered a glance her way and smiled a little. Apologetic, she guessed by the angle of his eyebrows. The older couple glanced over at her, too, offering polite expressions but nothing more. At least she didn't know them.

Resolutely, she turned away. Surely he wouldn't be talking forever.

At last, she heard him say, "Sorry. Happens sometimes, even on a day off."

Prepared with a forgiving smile, she gave it to him. "No worries. I run into folks sometimes, too. You don't get to avoid them, do you?"

His shake of the head was rueful, she decided. "No, not really. So. Are we ready?"

"As soon as we check out."

He cleared his throat when they reached the shortest available checkout line. "I wanted to apologize."

"For what?" she asked, moving her cart up a little and looking back at him at the same time. She thought she might have caught him studying her birthmark, but wasn't sure. Maybe he was checking her out? The idea made her blush and bite her lips together to keep from exploding in a smile. He appeared very serious and she wanted to respect that.

"I didn't introduce you."

She waved off the apology. "Why should you? For all intents and purposes," she rambled, borrowing a phrase from her father, "I'm just a furniture tech who's working at the church, right?" Didn't bother her in the least.

He came around his cart so that he was in front of it, and closer to her. "I don't want you to feel unimportant," he murmured, obviously not wanting to be overheard. Though how anyone could hear him in the crowd near the front of this place was beyond her. "I just didn't want you to have to deal with a bunch of questions or anything."

"Questions?"

Amused and even more intrigued, she watched as he mentally went through whatever series of things he considered saying to her. His mouth opened, closed, opened again. A slight smile tugged his lips up on one side. Careful, was what he was. Careful, concerned about appearances and order and what was *right*. She liked that. More than she thought she might. At last, he surprised and pleased her by covering her hand where it rested on the red handle of her shopping cart. "Never mind. Just remember it wasn't to exclude you or anything, all right?"

"Sure," she said softly. He removed his hand and she felt its absence more than was likely a good idea.

It was her turn to move forward now and she did so, still feeling the pressure of his hand on hers. He had the most electric effect on her. Unaccountably nervous, she paid for the water and other items in her cart and waited for Mark to do the same. It didn't take long before they were out the door and into the parking lot.

"Where's your car?" she asked him, taking her sunglasses from the bright red purse over her shoulder.

"Over there."

"Mine, too. Cool!"

They both chuckled when they saw that he had, unknowing, parked right next to her little yellow Mini. "You sure about this?" he asked as they loaded their purchases in their respective cars.

"Not planning on taking advantage of a blonde, are you?" she teased.

He smiled slowly, that deadly dimple barely visible, but still tempting for all that. "No."

"Then yes, I'm sure. I've even got a towel so you don't burn your legs on the front seat." He was wearing khaki shorts with a white polo shirt. "The leatherette stuff really absorbs the heat, if you haven't found that out yet."

"You weren't kidding about this preparation stuff, were you?"

"Nope. Do you have any shades?"

"Yeah," he said, ducking back into the front seat of his Camry and reappearing with a pair of sunglasses. "Here they are. Not real flashy, but they do the job."

"Hop in then, Mark, and we'll get going."

Her skin was humming with enthusiasm as he opened the passenger door and slid swiftly in. With a look, he silently asked if he could adjust the seat. She nodded, pleased that he felt comfortable enough to do so.

We could maybe be friends, she mused to herself, contented. *Mom always wanted that for me.*

It was strange, Mark admitted, but also fun, to be so firmly and laughingly compelled to engage in acts of tourism. It had been far too long since he had smiled as much as he was smiling now, cruising south toward Fort Myers Beach in a convertible, with the wind pushing his hair back and tugging at his collar. "This is great," he told Shelley.

She flashed him a smile. "I'm so glad. Now, over there," she said in a voice that sounded like she worked the Jungle Cruise at Walt Disney World or something, "you can see a delicious Caribbean restaurant."

"Caribbean? Haven't tried that."

She shot him a glance as they stopped at a red light. "Are you kidding? Never mind. I know. You're not. But Mark," she said while jiggling the gearshift, "you have *got* to get out more."

"Apparently. How about we go there for lunch?"

"Excellent."

Intense curiosity invaded his awareness. Curiosity about how this unusually enthusiastic young woman got to be this way. And, though he barely admitted it to himself as they moved ahead again with a green light and continued south, he wished that he had met someone like her years ago.

"You're a great tour guide," he informed her as they went across a fly-over that connected one street to another. "Have you lived here all your life? One of those—what do they call native Floridians?—Crackers?" He had seen that term on some of the local cars.

"Thanks!" She slowed, shifting smoothly as they hit a nearly empty straightaway. "No, I'm a transplant, like a lot of folks here. Once, at a Bible study at church, the teacher asked where we were each from. Only one-third of the class was actually born in Florida. And to be a Cracker, I think, is something like having to be here for generations. You know, the kind of family that can say, *'we came here before air conditioning.'* "

He chuckled in appreciation. "Where are you from, then?"

"South Carolina." The wind tossed the short sections of her hair playfully, and Mark was just enjoying the view as they passed trees, shops, and so much green grass for March. "Born and raised."

"When'd you come here?"

"After I graduated high school. Dad got a job with the company and we moved, he and I." Then she slowed down. Turning from watching her mobile expression, Mark looked ahead to see two lines of cars. And, far ahead, a traffic signal. Far, far ahead. Shelley made an impatient rapping sound on her steering wheel that shocked Mark out of proportion, for it was something he was prone to do himself. "Great," his tour guide snapped. "Now I remember why our singles' group at church never—but never—comes here 'til the first weekend in May."

The sun bounced off shiny sports cars, SUVs, sandy windshields, and chrome as the lanes rose to go over what looked like a bridge. "Ah," he remarked. "Spring break?"

"Yep."

"Well, it's a great day for it. And really, I'm not on a schedule today. Are you?"

She stopped beating out an impatient tattoo on her steering wheel. "You're right. It is and I'm not." Inhaling deeply, she relaxed against the back of her seat. "So. Where were we?"

"You were telling me about moving down here. You and your dad."

"Oh, yeah. So we came down after my brother left for college. He started off by doing service calls like I do now, and I worked in the warehouse on the furniture. Now, he manages the warehouse and I do calls." Shelley's grin was infectious. He smiled, too, as they moved slowly forward with the lines of cars. "It's been a good life."

"You said, I think, that you never went to college?"

"Nah. I didn't. I mean, why? I have a job that I make pretty good money at, you know? I like it. I'll probably be able to do it until I retire, so why spend the money going to school? My brother, though," she went on with a sly sideways smile at him, "went to Arizona State."

"Is he older or younger than you?" That intense curiosity was still with him.

"Older."

"What's he do now?"

She laughed. "Oh, right. Um, do you watch baseball at all? The Majors?"

"Sometimes . . ."

"He plays second base for the Arizona Diamondbacks," Shelley declared proudly with a full look at him. Probably, Mark guessed, to gauge his reaction.

Suitably impressed, he nodded. "That's great. Must be a lot of fun for all of you."

"You ever go to a game in a big stadium?" Then, before he could answer, she held up one hand. "Never mind. I bet the answer is no."

He laughed. "You're right."

"Okay, your turn," she declared as they reached—at last—the traffic light and had a view of the bridge and Fort Myers Beach.

"My turn?" The light turned green and he kept quiet as Shelley expertly maneuvered her way into the traffic heading to the beach. The kids he saw all looked like they were maybe undergrads in college. He saw a couple of college banners, too. Bikini tops. Board shorts. Sunburns. The wind grew more insistent as they got to the other side of the bridge and to the island itself. And there, Mark saw what seemed to him to be a scene out of some movie. Young people in their beachwear, older people with fishing hats. Buildings in bright pinks, blues, and yellows. Pedestrians everywhere and, when he inhaled deeply, the scent of frying pastry. Not salt, which he had expected, but *food*. "Where do you park around here?" he wondered aloud.

"I have this great space I usually try for. It's a little complicated, but we'll make it eventually. It's shaded."

"Shade is good," he remarked, watching the people with their beach gear and beverages maneuver around the slowly moving vehicles. Everyone was very polite, he decided. No honking horns, no obscenities. Just people out to enjoy themselves and not bother anyone.

After ducking around a trio of young men—who eyed Shelley with an appreciation that Mark recognized in his gut—they pulled under an overpass, where a little booth with an orange traffic flag announced all day parking for two dollars. "Here we are," Shelley announced. "Now. I'm going to put the top up, so . . ."

"I'm out, I'm out," Mark said with a chuckle, pushing himself out of the car and stretching. "Where are we going now, Tour Guide Shelley?"

Slinging her red purse over her shoulder, she said, "The Pier. You have to see The Pier."

It was the first thing he had seen as they had crossed the bridge, but he understood. "Lead the way."

Together, they took their turn as pedestrians, avoiding the cars, hurrying across narrow lanes to a colorful little area with shops and something that he thought was supposed to be Blues music but just sounded like revamped elevator Muzak. The aroma of the pastries, though, was all around, as were the kitschy souvenir vendors and small bistro tables with enormous blue umbrellas. Listening, he heard smatterings of Spanish and German as well as some other European tongues. Not to mention the slangy conversations of American college students on their spring break vacations. And there, just at the foot of the bridge, was the ubiquitous Dairy Queen.

"Why am I not surprised?" he murmured with a shake of his head.

Once out on the narrow bridge that led to The Pier, he was not really able to talk to Shelley at all, since there was a traffic pattern that admitted precisely one person in each direction. However, he was more than able to enjoy the fresh winds and salty Gulf of Mexico smells. Pelicans swooped dangerously low to dive into the water, and fishermen inhabited the bump-outs around the souvenir shop/coffee bar and at the end of The Pier itself.

Once they got to the final platform, Shelley leaned against the wooden railing and grinned up at him. "It's your turn now," she reminded him.

Enjoying the way the wind played with her sun-bright hair, he indicated with a motion of his hand that she could ask away. She plied him with questions of her own, ranging from where he was from, where he went to college, what had he studied, had he been married before . . .

He blinked. "No, I haven't."

"Come close?" she inquired with a teasing lilt to her voice that carried strangely through the wind to his ears.

It was impossible to be offended by her persistence. Maybe it was the angle of her head or that curl in her voice. "Maybe," he allowed, leaning his elbows on the railing and looking out over the rapidly filling white sand beach not far from them. The only problem with this position was that it put him rather close to a bare, tanned shoulder, and he had to force himself not to trace its curve with his eyes. He had a list of reasons why he shouldn't be doing that, but the biggest one was that Shelley had made it very clear that they were bartering. This wasn't anything more than a give and take.

She blurred that impression in the next breath. "You were close to getting married? And they let you get *away*?"

A burst of warmth erupted under his skin and he had to laugh.

She buried her face in her hands, shoulders shaking with silent laughter. "Sorry," she managed, the word barely carrying to him.

He tugged one of her hands down so he could take off her sunglasses and see her face. She didn't try to stop him. "Hey. Don't be." A huge pressure seemed suddenly to overshadow them and he couldn't move. As if all that was required, just this minute, was to surround himself in the brown lights that danced in Shelley's eyes. She had such a life about her. A life that he hadn't really known he had been missing until he met her.

The moment ended as such moments tended to end. Her sunglasses fell from his fingers, landing on the wooden slats at their feet. She reacted more rapidly than he, dropping down to the floor of The Pier and snatching up the glasses on her smooth ascent. They were on her face before he knew it, and so was her smile.

"C'mon," she said, sounding breathless. Maybe it was his imagination, maybe it was the wind, but he did think she sounded breathless. "You haven't walked on the beach yet and you really need to, if you're going to be a tourist."

A tourist he was, then, for the remainder of their time at Fort Myers Beach. She pointed out Sanibel from where they were on Bowditch Point. Showed him the parasailing craft. He saw hotels and beach villas and apartments that looked out over the Gulf, and was able to stand right next to a pelican resting on a dock that was marked as a Manatee Area. All in all, it was an experience that he would have been sorry to have missed.

Even if it left him feeling confused. Shelley had been the one to initiate this excursion, seemed to enjoy his company, but she pulled away from his gaze, his proximity, every time he thought that maybe, maybe, she was moving beyond the idea of "bartering".

God was trying to tell him something, Mark was pretty sure. But what?

At length, they made their way to her clever parking space under the overpass and decided it was time for lunch at the Caribbean restaurant Shelley had mentioned on their trip down. "They have the *best* lemonade," she told him.

Leaving the top to the Mini up, due to one set of rather pink shoulders, they returned over the bridge and past the greenery into Fort Myers and the Caribbean place. The lemonade was even better than Shelley had promised, and the cool, shady interior was ideal after a windblown morning spent at the beach.

"You're a terrific tour guide," he told her.

"Thank you. I'm having a blast."

He paused a moment and then decided to take a leap of faith. "Want to do this again? I mean," he added quickly, so she didn't feel compelled to turn him down because this wasn't, he remembered clearly, a *date*, "that I have some friends coming out from California on a second honeymoon and they wanted to get together."

"Oh! Excellent. Yes. You have to take them to that seafood place on the river," she gushed, leaning forward over her empty plate. "Absolutely *must*."

He regretted it when the check arrived. Out came his wallet, but she held up one hand and took the bill. They discussed it, both with their tongues thoroughly in cheek, and went Dutch. He had never had so much fun arguing over a bill before.

"Do you drive a stick?" she asked him, fishing her keys from the shiny red purse.

Going down a small set of three steps toward the exterior door of the restaurant, he told her he did and was amazed when she tossed him her keys. "Then you can take us back to Costco."

Still in a bit of shock about that, he held the door open for her to leave and happened to look up, just for a final impression of the place. "I think I'll recommend this to my friends," he told Shelley. In answer to the delighted light in her eyes, he added, "If only for the lemonade."

Then, he saw a silver head pop out of a large booth off to his right. And another, and another. Seven in all, looking like a group of meerkats he had once seen on cable. The Naomi Circle, a Bible study group at church, was apparently having their monthly luncheon here. Today. And they were all beaming at him with maternal approval.

Oh, great.

Five

"You mostly like playing baseball with your brother, when he lets you."

"So, yeah, it's been good that I took all that Spanish, you know. We have these Mexican teams up to play us this week in Tucson, Shell. And let me tell you, these boys bring their A game," Stevie Roberts, second baseman for the Arizona Diamondbacks, told her through his webcam. "Okay. It's getting dark over there in South Florida, sis. Turn on a light or something. I can hardly see you."

Next to the sofa was a floor lamp that swung out over the soft expanse on a squared angle. Shelley turned it on. "It's all of half past eight, guy. Gimme a break."

He leaned forward into his camera and stared. "Shell? Do you have some kind of filter on your webcam or something? You're all pink."

She sighed a little and winced. She was wearing the absolute bare minimum around her face and shoulders. "Got a little sunburned today, Stevie. Took an unplanned trip to the beach."

The well-built baseball player with a thatch of blond hair leaned back from his computer. "Ouch. Sorry. Looks painful. Was it worth it?"

She grinned at him. "Every minute. Definitely."

His face assumed a hideous, fraternal aspect as he lifted one brow in playful superiority. "So . . ."

"Oh no, not again."

"What?" he demanded, spreading his hands apologetically. "I'm in Arizona. What'm I gonna do this time?"

"Uh-huh. No, thanks. I know better. I was apologizing for you for weeks, last time."

"Does he at least have a first name?"

"Mark."

"Does he have a job?"

She laughed. Her family was always so worried about her. "Yes."

"Doing . . . what? A driver at the warehouse? Electrician? Roofer? Pool guy?"

"A pool guy. Now wouldn't *that* be interesting?" she teased. "None of the above, Stevie. I promise though, that if you get to meet him, I'll tell you. Deal?"

"Invite him to that game in July, when we play the Marlins."

"Does Dad have tickets?"

"Yep."

"Well then, if he's around, I'll do that. I'm kind of his tour guide, I think, and he's never seen a stadium game in person before."

"Go get some of that gunk on your shoulders, Shell. I'm serious. You look terrible."

"Thanks a lot. I will. Have a good night."

"You, too."

Tuesday at The Empty, Dinah mainly focused on Shelley's sunburn. In the warehouse, her father sent her a raised brow and said, "I talked to your brother, you know."

Shifting her map book under her arm, Shelley shook her head. "Yeah, yeah. Is he ratting on me?"

Dad chuckled. "Nope. Just said you'd had . . . a busy day."

"We are a fine family for understatement."

"We are. But Shelley?"

As his tone had shifted, so did her focus on him. "Yeah, Dad?"

He ruffled her hair with one work-hardened hand. "Be careful, all right?"

Impulsively, she kissed his cheek. "I will. Promise. Have a good one."

On her way out, she checked once more with Dinah. "Can I see my call list for tomorrow?"

"You betcha. You've got a whopping one call. You're going back to that church. The to-do list is pretty long." She handed the work order up to Shelley and took a sip of her tea. "Pages. Did someone go in there with a knife or something?"

"Shh, don't tell anyone, but it was The Masked Delivery Team."

"Ah."

"Yeah. So, make sure those parts are pulled and all that, all right? I don't want to be late."

"Hey, wait a minute!"

Shelley stopped and turned on the heel of her work boots. "What?"

"Isn't this the place where that TDH is?"

With a wink, Shelley turned again. "I'll never tell."

The following morning, she woke with a huge enthusiasm for her job. If she completed the call today—a large task, considering there were so many pieces and it was going to take her pretty much all day—then Dr. Mark Countryman would no longer be a customer, but a former customer. And that, really, made all the difference, didn't it?

They had been able to talk easily, for the most part, about almost anything. Her mom had said that was something she and Dad had been able to do. Shelley felt her own smile as she made her coffee, and didn't hold it back at all.

Since it was going to be a long day, she prepared at home. She would need a cooler, for sure. A soda or two, bottled water, and some finger foods. She preferred apple slices, crackers, and some string cheese, all tucked away on ice in the cooler. Hand wipes, too. She would also need to make sure to check her rollaway box. Today she would need all of her stains and tools, and it was most convenient to carry them about in the huge plastic box she had outfitted for the purpose.

With the cooler in the Mini, she took off to work, picked up the bits and pieces she needed at The Empty, and ran through the call in her head. Her father found her a bit preoccupied, but didn't comment beyond, "Drive safe, Shell."

"Will do, Dad."

Doing a return call was always a little tricky. She had visited before and had presumably come away with a thorough understanding of the furniture and the requirements for fixing *everything* to a customer's satisfaction. At least, that's the way it was often interpreted by the customer. The service techs knew that sometimes things just happened and another call would be required, and so on. There was generally no charge to the customer, if the pieces were under warranty, but they did not appreciate it when the work was still undone when she left.

Then, too, a return call allowed her to pray more comprehensively for the customer. She had met them, sometimes, so she had a face in mind when she prayed. Today, she had several faces. Senior Pastor with the enormous bookcase and matching leather chairs. Youth Pastor with the dings on the table legs and scratched bookshelves. Children's Pastor with the uneven legs on the desk, the odd arm on her new chair and a rather large dent in her bookcase. And, of course, Dr. Countryman. *Mark*.

"So, do I want to start at Mark's office, or end there? That's the question," she murmured with a smile as she pulled into the church's parking lot. Since she was going to be there all day, she felt it wouldn't be right to block their drop-off point outside the front door.

She set her cooler in the back of the company van after lugging her workbox out, rolling it once, to make sure all was in order. It was. Then, camera and phone in their customary places, Shelley pulled the box behind her up the walk and into the church foyer.

And no one was there. The door had been open, but no one was at the front desk. She knew her way though, so called out. "Hello? It's Shelley Roberts to work on the new furniture?" Her voice echoed until, finally, she heard someone.

"Yes. Good morning. It's early." From the office marked *Senior Pastor, Benjamin Keller*, there was a light shining and a friendly voice. Then, there was the man himself, dressed in a pair of slacks and dress shirt, but no tie. "Shelley, right? Good to see you again."

"Good morning, sir. Um, should I start in your office or would it be better to leave you be and work in someone else's to get started?"

"Here's fine, if you like. Need me to move anything?"

She waved off the idea with a smile. "Not just now. I'll go ahead and get started. Where are your electrical outlets?"

Doing burn-ins for the dings in the wood, Shelley was happy to tell Pastor Keller about each step of the procedure, since he seemed interested. He had a terrific voice and she enjoyed hearing him tell stories, too, about a Day in the Life. She did the same, making him laugh with anecdotes about the unusual moments about the job.

"What're you doing now?" he inquired a couple of hours later, as she was doing the final touches on the top of the desk.

She glanced to where he was sitting on a red leather chair, laptop computer angled awkwardly on his knees. "Drawing."

His chuckle was sincere. "Drawing on my new desk?"

"Oh, yeah. How else do you think I'll be able to reproduce all these grain markings?"

He shifted the laptop and rose. "Are you serious?"

She showed him how she used the graining marker to reproduce the woodgrain on the surface of the desk. "All part of the service," she quipped, leaning this way and that to make sure it looked acceptable from different angles. "Look okay?"

His face displayed wondering humor. "Wow. I am impressed." He crouched. "You can't even tell." Standing again, he grinned. "I see why Jacob Cairns asked for you."

She felt the blood rush to her face and immediately ducked to return all of her paraphernalia to the workbox. "Well, thank you. It's my job. I guess I'll be heading down the hall. Let me know if you catch anything irregular while I'm still here. I'll come back and see what I can do."

Maneuvering her workbox, she left Pastor Keller's office and had to make a decision. She had been shown the pieces in Customer Cairns' own personal order of priority. Deciding that was a decent guide, she smiled, shook her head at herself, and turned to go to Mark's door.

"Hello?" she called, smiling a little as she poked her head into the office. He had left the door open.

Wearing a striped dress shirt and dark slacks, he looked like he could have stepped out of an advertisement. "Shelley, hello!" Then, his eyes narrowed in a studious manner and he beckoned to her to come a bit closer. "You look like you've seen some sun since the last time you were here."

She angled a brow at him. "Ya think, Dr. Countryman?"

"Seriously," he said, his voice low. "You all right? You were getting pretty burned." His hand came up, as if he'd brush her cheek with his fingers. She held her breath, but he seemed to think better of it and made an awkward "hand through the hair" transition.

She pretended it never happened. "That's what my brother said, too. He thought I put a filter on my webcam. I'm fine now, though. I've got one of those complexions that goes from pink to tan." She grinned at him and arranged her workbox. "So. Thank you for getting the books off the shelving. If you need me to leave at any point, let me know, okay? I know that you pastor-types have different job requirements."

He shook his head, a smile lurking in his brilliant black eyes. "All I'm doing is polishing my lesson for tonight."

"Cool. I'll try not to bother you," she assured him. "Be right back." She was thirsty and thought she'd raid her cooler before starting on Mark's office. On her way back, she was met by the Children's Minister.

"Oh, hi! Am I next?" The other woman's smile was anticipatory, her high voice polite.

"I'm just starting in Dr. Countryman's office, but you're after that."

"Great. Hey, I'm going to be going out for some lunch in a bit. Can I get you anything?"

Shelley smiled. "No, thank you. I'm fine."

"Okay. See you in a bit."

A bit was probably going to turn out to be more like an hour or so, Shelley reflected as she reached Mark's office again. "I'm back. And, I'm going to have to ask you to move off to one side of your desk, if that's all right. I want to check that drawer glide first."

"Uh, sure," he said, wheeling his chair over a little.

It was disconcerting to be situated so closely to him. He was, of course, diligently working at his keyboard, but she felt his eyes on her a couple of times as she made some adjustments and put the rubber bumper on the glide to stop the annoying metallic sound that had so irritated Customer Cairns. She felt really on edge, actually. The sensation was not in any way alleviated by the similar feeling she was picking up on the other side of the desk, less than three feet from her.

Was she making him uncomfortable in a bad way? Did he wish they hadn't gone to the beach together? She couldn't ask, and the increasingly heavy silence was driving her crazy.

I have to work on this. Find something to talk about. All right, Shell. Where's your famous scintillating personality, huh? C'mon, already!

Her mind was still agitating with a lopsided spin, like a broken washing machine, trying to find something to talk about that had *nothing whatsoever* to do with their day at Fort Myers Beach or the lunch that followed. She was at work now, and she had to be a professional.

"You said you liked the book of James?"

His question reached her like a sturdy rope. "Yes." She practically gasped, feeling stupid but also relieved beyond measure that he had found something to say. "You've got a good memory."

"I try," he said, smiling easily.

She checked and yes, the killer dimple was in evidence. She wanted to touch it. *Shell, behave!*

He continued. "I'm actually teaching on that book starting after Easter."

"Oh?"

"Yes, for Wednesday night Bible study. If, you know, you want to come."

"Would I have to sign up in advance or anything?"

"Not at all, no pressure. Just wanted you to know."

"Well, thank you." She grinned at him and then hurried to try to back up and move around his desk. Which, of course, was why it was her turn to run into a spot of dense gravity. "Yawp," she blurted.

"Shelley!" He tried to reach her, she knew he did, but he didn't quite make it before she hit the floor.

She was more amused than anything and the laughter wasn't about to go away when she registered the chagrin, concern, and wry amusement that flickered over his features. "Gravity Well. What'd I tell you?"

He laughed with more amusement than the joke probably warranted, but that was fine with her. He had a great laugh. She sighed a little.

"Everything okay?"

Shelley was just regaining her feet when she saw four people trying to get through one doorway. "I'm fine. Just fell, is all."

"Gravity Well," Mark said sagely.

"Uh-huh. So long as you're all right. We don't want a lawsuit."

"No worries. I'm fine, honest."

Eventually they left and she was able to get back to work, with nary a rug burn to show for it.

She fixed his bookshelves, surprised him—as she had the Senior Pastor—with her work on the woodgrain, and had him laughing about The Empty at the warehouse, as well as some of the anecdotes she had shared with Pastor Keller down the hall.

When she was just about done with all the pieces in his office, he smiled a little. "So, are you allowed to get tips when you do a call?"

She blushed a little. "Yeah, but we usually don't talk about it." To redirect her embarrassment, she said, "You would not believe some of the stuff people have given me or tried to give me."

"Like what?"

"Oh, a fifth of Jack Daniels once. Can you believe it?"

He gaped and then laughed. "You're kidding."

Ah, the dimple... "Scout's honor. Got some Belgian chocolate once, too. And someone else gave me something she had made. A real nice crocheted throw." She smiled a little. "My mom taught me how to crochet, so I've got a lot of throws, but it was really nice of the lady."

"I don't think I've heard you mention your mother before," Mark said, the laughter out of his voice but the smile still lingering as she met his gaze. "Where is she?"

With a small smile, she instinctively touched the small pink ribbon pin she wore on the collar of her midnight blue shirt. "She died when I was ten. Breast cancer." It was still a sorrow, but the question had been asked often enough that she could answer it without pain.

"Aw, Shelley. I'm sorry. I didn't know." He seemed about to extend a hand to her, thought better of it, and leaned against his desk. "I'm sorry." It was just the right amount of "sorry", she felt. But then, he was a minister, right? This was probably something he had a lot of practice with.

"Thank you." Then, to bring the smile back, she pointed at his desk. "Careful! You don't want any of that stuff on your pants."

It worked. He was still chuckling as she wheeled her workbox out of his office and down to the Children's Minister's. "Hello. You ready for me?"

With some trips out to the van for a drink or something to eat when she felt she had to, as well as to retrieve a couple of different tools and a polishing cloth, Shelley finished the final two offices much in the same way as she had the first two. Some of the stories were the same, and they always got a laugh. She had to wonder, as she finished up in the Youth Pastor's office, if they'd all be comparing notes later. At least she had been consistent.

Shelley had arrived a little after eight in the morning. When she finished with the final piece in the final office, she made a quick trip through all the rest. "Everything all right?" she asked the Children's Minister. "Holding up okay?" she inquired of the Senior Pastor. She ended with Mark's office. "I think I'm done," she told him with a smile. "It's about three and I'm ready for lunch."

"Hey, we tried to feed you," he said, going to one of the cardboard boxes in his office. "I heard at least three people ask you if you wanted some lunch."

"You're all very kind," she assured him, wishing she could lean against the door. But no, she was working. "So. Everything all right?"

"Yep. And here. It's not a crocheted blanket or anything," he said, with half a shrug that Shelley found adorable, "but it *is* something I made—sort of—and I thought it might come in handy."

It was a book. *Timeless in a Changing Age* by Dr. Mark Countryman. "Wow, you wrote a book? You didn't tell me that."

"Are you impressed?" he asked on a laugh.

"Yes! Excellent." She turned it over and skimmed the back cover, learning that it was a book about teaching the Bible in the changing contemporary climate. "Wow, Ma—Dr. Countryman. Thank you so much."

"If you have any questions about it," he said, offering her a business card, "here's my contact information." He leaned in a little and said, very conspiratorially, "I haven't forgotten my half of our deal."

Despite the sudden increase in her heart rate, she laughed softly. "I'll certainly read it. And, um, thanks for the tip." It was hard, when it came down to it, to leave the office. But she managed, holding her hand out to shake his as she had when she had first walked in the week before. "I'll just have Pastor Keller sign off on all of this then, and I'll be out of everyone's hair." Without giving him a chance to say anything else—she was feeling awkward enough—she left to return to the Senior Pastor's office.

"Sir? If I could have you sign off that everything has been completed to your satisfaction, I can leave you all in peace," she said, holding up her clipboard with the voluminous work order.

"Ah. Already?"

She grinned. "It is after three, sir. Yep, *already*."

"Well then, let's take a look."

He crossed to her to take her clipboard and noticed the book. "What's that?"

Trying not to blush, she told him, "A tip. Did I tell you about the whiskey someone tried to offer me once? This is way better."

His salt-and-pepper eyebrows bushed up into his forehead. "Ah. Yes, indeed. Of course. So, let's go take a look at this stuff, hmm?"

She left the book on her workbox and followed Pastor Keller around from office to office as he inspected her work. She wasn't nervous, but she did want to make a favorable impression on everyone and hoped that he would sign off and she would have a complete call.

He had her explain something in almost every office, though, and she did. It wasn't until she had gathered all her equipment, and returned to the van that she found out what Pastor Keller had been up to during that inspection.

Four ten-dollar bills slipped out of Mark's book to flutter to her feet. She blushed all over.

"Shelley!"

Kneeling to pick up the money, Shelley was still half-laughing at the cagey senior pastor when Mark reached her. "All done?" he asked.

"Yes. And please, Dr. Countryman, tell everyone thank you for me, would you? They're really too generous."

"Are you still working?"

"Nope, I'm now officially on my lunch."

He smiled. "Good. So please, call me Mark, all right?"

"Yes, sir. Mark. Yes. Okay."

"Good. And if you're not working, can I get your, ah, contact information, too? I have those friends coming in, you might remember, and I might need some more tourist advice."

She blinked in surprise, but nodded. Now that she was off-duty, she felt quite self-conscious in turning her back to him and bending to reach into the van to get a business card. Her skin felt hot and her fingers trembled a bit. *Stop it. Just stop it. He wants your phone number, Shell. You can do this.*

Turning back to him, she saw that he was leaning against the van, his focus on the church building. *Well, that's good, I guess, that he wasn't staring at my backside.* "Here," she said, trying to sound casual. "E-mail is here, and . . . I wrote down my personal cell. We can't put our work cells on there, since customers aren't supposed to be able to contact us individually."

He had pushed himself off the van and was standing in front of her, very focused on her eyes. "Shelley . . . " She waited, eyebrows raised, but he just shook his head. "Never mind. Thank you."

"You're welcome."

Six

"Find a man that is a friend, in addition to all the rest . . ."

"Yeah, the new place is coming along, Mom, thanks. I'd love to have you guys come on out, when you feel you can." He was sitting on a lawn chair on The Walk, next to the Caloosahatchee, completely enjoying the light breeze and the sunset, as it came in over the river. It was Thursday, he had had a good day, and he was thinking that he wanted to call Shelley in a while, about the tourist stuff for Garrison and Dawn, of course.

"That would be great, but I think we'll wait until the autumn, dear. You guys are already getting into the warmer weather and, frankly, your dad and I would rather not have to worry about hurricanes."

Mark sighed and shook his head. "There's been barely a tropical storm since I got here, Mom. But, if it'll make you feel any better, I'm bartering." There was that word again, and Mark blessed Shelley for coming up with it.

"Bartering?"

"With a local, actually. About that kind of thing. She's already started telling me about hurricane preparation."

"Ah, a local lady? Well, that's a relief. A member of your church?"

"No, she's a girl I just ran into one day."

His mother, ensconced with a cup of tea in the Big Sur region of California, laughed out loud. "Ran into? You? Was she injured?"

"Not that kind of thing, Mom. Actually, you might appreciate the fact that she kept me from falling into a Gravity Well."

"A what?"

He chuckled. "That's what she calls them, anyway."

"Well, Mark, I'm definitely intrigued. You'll have to keep me posted."

"Will do. Hey, I'm going to give her a call, so if you'll excuse me . . ."

"Of course. And Mark?"

He knew that tone of voice, was a bit wary of it—for he still didn't feel he had a clear path ahead of him—but he still said, "What, Mom?"

"You know, if she's willing to take the time with you and all . . . You might consider more than bartering."

"Mom. Enough."

Ending the conversation with his mother, Mark was smiling to himself. And feeling nervous. Which was probably ridiculous, but still—

He prayed again not to misread the situation, and asked the Lord to guard his steps and actions and words. Living alone as he did but wishing he didn't, it was too easy to see more than there was, or try to make something out of nothing. He didn't want to do that again. "Quit delaying. It's an easy question," he told himself bracingly.

Hadn't he placed his life in God's hands in total faith a long time ago? *Yes.* And though he hadn't emerged from his experiences unscathed, he still had faith. Faith to see him through any circumstance. *So call her, already.*

Pulling her card from a pocket, he dialed her number and hit Send.

"Hello?" It was her voice, sounding a little strained.

"Shelley? It's Mark."

There was a change in the background sounds on her end. "Oh, hi! Good to hear from you. I am *so* enjoying your book."

He shook his head with a smile at the river. "You only just got it."

"Fast reader. Honest. Hang on. Let me just maneuver."

"Everything all right?"

It was silent save for her voice when she answered. "Definitely. Just, um, working on a project. So, what's up? How was your lesson last night? How's everyone at the office?"

"Slow down." Laughing, he rose and swung his chair up, too, before heading up the mild rise of lush green grass to his own door. "Everything's great. Everyone is fine. Ben particularly enjoyed, ah, your work yesterday." He did not tell her of the mild teasing he had been subject to at the weekly staff meeting that morning. It wasn't something he wanted her to be concerned about. Like the not-so-subtle questions Wednesday evening about the "nice girl" he had been seen with at lunch on Monday, and so on. Good women, all, the Naomi Circle. They had only wanted to tell him that his "lady friend" had seemed engaging and where did she go to church?

Shelley really didn't need to hear that. It had been hard on Christina, that was for sure.

A notable lessening of vocal tension came through when she resumed their conversation. "Okay. So. What's up?"

"Well, it's about my friends coming in from California."

"Oh, yeah. You do know which restaurant I was referring to the other day, don't you?"

"The one at the hotel? It's just down The Walk from me, so yes."

"Ah, good. I'm so glad you know it. Make sure to have them try the blackened grouper. Can't come to Florida and not have it."

Well, here goes. Worst that can happen is she'll say no. "Would you be interested in telling them this yourself? They'll be here the week between Palm Sunday and Easter, and they want to get together at some point. Thought I'd try that place. Would you like to join me?" A pause.

"Um, are you asking me out?"

Was he? When he had asked her the same question, she had answered in the negative. He did want to wait for God's leading, but how could he know without trying to move forward, step by step? It was on the tip of his tongue to say that he was indeed asking her out, when she jumped in again.

"I know. These are your friends, right? And you don't want to be The Single Guy." He could hear the capital letters when she spoke and, in spite of the fact that she wasn't exactly on target, he had to smile at her perspicacity; Dawn *had* wanted a double date, after all. "So you need a date for the evening? Sure! I can do that."

He closed his eyes and leaned against the door, smiling a little helplessly. "You sure? I don't want you to feel awkward."

"Me?" She laughed—a rich sound that went from his ear to his heart, warming him considerably. "When you do what I do, Mark, being awkward happens a lot, but I'll make sure that no one—not even you—knows it."

"Well, I look forward to it. Not to your being awkward, of course, but to having dinner with you. And Garrison and Dawn. I'm not sure which night will work for them, though."

"Hey, I've got all week open, as far as I know. Except Wednesday. Bible Study. But otherwise, we're on, all right?"

"All right. And thank you."

Tuesday was the designated day. Following her directions, Mark drove to an older neighborhood in North Fort Myers. The fading sunlight caught on numerous For Sale signs and there were frequent indicators of neglect on her street. Like many places in South Florida, the downturn in the economy had hit this neighborhood hard. Her house was on the corner. *"Big tree,"* she had told him. *"And a small picket fence."*

There it was, and he pulled into the narrow drive. Smallish house, he supposed, but his place was smaller. The corner lot was nice. Lots of greenery as he walked to the door and rang the bell.

The door opened outward, as most of them seemed to in the area. He was still getting used to that, even after the nearly three years he had lived here. "Hello!"

"Hello to you, too," he said. "Ready?"

"Just a sec. Want to come in? I have to find my shoes. Hey, nice shirt."

Stepping in, he was pleased to know his choice of shirt met with her approval. The restaurant was a casual place, so he had chosen a bar-striped shirt over a pair of jeans and sneakers. They would be eating practically on the water, with the walls rolled up to let in the evening air, he was guessing, as the establishment tended to do that when the weather was fine. "Thanks. Yes, I think shoes would be good. What happened?"

She gestured vaguely at a sofa in her living room. Looked expensive, but then she did work for a store that specialized in good furniture. He didn't want to sit down, appealing as the bright accent pillows looked in here.

She disappeared down a hallway, her voice echoing back to him. "I was looking for the sandals that go with this top. They've got these little bows on them and I really want to wear them."

A man could not argue with a woman and her footwear, so Mark resigned himself to looking around the living room while he waited.

There were some family pictures on the walls, a flat-screen television, and one wall had a series of bookcases under the windows. Row upon row of books. His, though, was on the sofa, not on a shelf. That pleased him. Good to know she was really reading it.

"Okay. I think I'm ready. Will I embarrass you in front of your friends?" She grinned and turned around, the bottom of her loose top flaring out over the jeans. The top itself went to her hips and was of some light, soft floral pattern, with ties at the back for shaping, he guessed. The sandals she had been looking for peeked out at the bottom of the jeans. "Glad you wore jeans, too. I just thought it'd be awful if we wound up at one of those high tables, you know, and I'd have to perch there in a dress."

"You look great, Shelley. You couldn't possibly embarrass me."

"Well, you know, you *are* a published author and everything, with that heavy Doctor of Theology title following you around," she teased him, turning off the lights as he opened the front door. "Didn't want to make you look bad."

He told her a little about Garrison and Dawn as they drove to the restaurant. When they reached the parking lot, he called Garrison to let them know he and Shelley had arrived. The restaurant was actually at the hotel, with a separate walk and dock, and Garrison had said they'd just come down to meet them.

Unexpectedly, Shelley took his hand. He glanced at her in surprise, but she just grinned up at him. "I'm a good date," she whispered. Mark was still chuckling when Garrison called his name.

"Good to see you."

He and Shelley shook hands all around as he introduced her. It *was* gratifying, he had to confess, to have someone at his side this evening. A pretended double date or not, it still felt good.

And it turned out that Shelley had chosen wisely. They were perched at the higher table overlooking the Caloosahatchee, with sodas in front of them and their orders placed, before he felt able to relax a little. Garrison was looking very content these days, and Dawn, well, Dawn would always be lovely. She had that kind of face. Mark was just thankful that there was no awkwardness whatsoever in this meeting of old friends.

He and Garrison discussed the church back in Glencoe while the women talked beside them. Garrison asked, "So, is she your local color adviser, Mark? She's got good taste."

"She is and she does."

"She is the one you mentioned, right?"

Mark felt color rise under his skin. "Yes."

"She reminds me of someone . . ."

They were going to continue that conversation when the words "hurricane season" slipped into their hearing, and Mark said, "Oh, no. Here she goes again," in what he hoped was a humorous way.

Dawn smiled. "Hey, after what she and her dad went through, maybe you should listen to her, Mark."

"The girls do stick together," Garrison murmured.

Shelley angled a brow at him. *Very effective, that.* "You only have to lose your roof once, you know, to make sure that if it happens again, you'll be ready. Being without power for a week and a half is a good motivator, too."

His eyes widened. He had never actually inquired about her previous hurricane experience, but had just figured she was one of those people who like to be ready for every contingency. She was, yes, but for good reason, it seemed. "It is. So you can help me get some supplies in, all right?"

"Thank you," she said with the air of *Finally!* in her expression and voice. Garrison and Dawn laughed.

Over dinner, Shelley fielded questions like a pro. "Oh, we met at a Chinese take-out. He fell right into my hands," she said with a grin at him.

Dawn shook her head so that her fair hair ruffled around her face. "What?"

"I kept him from losing his lunch and everything."

Garrison just stared.

"It's all true." Mark assured them with a nod. "Every word. And then she dragged me all over Fort Myers Beach—"

"I did not. You *walked*. And then we previewed another place you two *have* to go while you're down here. Best lemonade in the world."

Mark enjoyed himself a great deal, resting on his elbows after they had finished eating, and allowing himself to think that yes, it did feel like a real date, after all.

After they had finished and were standing around in that in-between social place between "party's over" and "goodbye", Dawn pulled him aside.

"Mark, I don't know when I've heard or seen you laugh more. If it's Shelley's doing, then you hang on to her, okay? She's a keeper." They glanced over to where Shelley was nodding at something Garrison was saying. Probably a story of his own, judging by his expression. *Maybe about the school where he taught or about his daughter, who was, come to think of it, near Shelley's age by now. Wow.*

Disconcerted, Mark absently accepted Shelley's hand when she slid it in his as Garrison and Dawn walked off into the moonlit night.

"You said they were on a second honeymoon, or something?" Shelley murmured as they moved slowly back to his car. "They totally look it. That's so sweet. How long have they been married?"

"Well, that's a long story," Mark said, bringing himself away from his sudden odd feeling about Shelley's age. "But I think this is their ninth anniversary."

"Ninth? Dawn was saying something about their daughter and it sounded like she was just a little younger than I am." The marked brown brows frowned a little, visible even in the uncertain light.

"Like I said, a long story."

"Ah. Okay."

It was. Garrison and Dawn had a long history, sometimes painful, but ultimately one of love. After what had happened between them when Garrison and Dawn had been in high school, it had taken the obvious machinations of the daughter they shared to bring the parents together again. "They are, though, the best example of forgiveness," was what he told Shelley as they strolled back to his car, prompted by something he didn't quite understand. "And they're good friends. Not just of mine, but also of one another."

She smiled up at him, the white light of the moon bathing her hair so that it looked much lighter than normal. "I'd like to think we're good friends," she told him, her tone sprightly and hopeful. "You and me, I mean. Think we could manage that?"

Ouch.

It was a palpable hit, but Mark took it like a man, he hoped, and smiled a little. Maybe it was all for the best. "I think we could, Shelley, yes."

"Oh, *good.*" Beaming, she took both his hands in hers and rolled up on her toes. "Because I think we make a great team."

As he drove her home, she was saying how much she had enjoyed meeting his friends. "I think, you know, from a feminine perspective, that Garrison Chase looks older than you by at least five years."

Distracted and still processing, Mark asked, "Why would you think that?"

"Receding hairline," Shelley answered, her voice conspiratorial. "But then," she went on, "he *has* been through the hazards of raising a teenage daughter, so maybe that accounts for it. My dad said I'm the reason he started going bald early."

He had to laugh at that. "You? Were you one of those really popular girls that had your dad watching the clock every night?"

"Me? Not even close. No. Dad used to call me a flirt," she confided.

"A flirt?" He remembered his initial impression of her and smiled. "Do you think you were?"

She stretched out a little and sighed, as if in pleasure. "Well. I think that for me it means I want people to feel good about being with me, you know? If that's flirting, then I'm a flirt. Which is what I told my dad."

He pulled into her driveway and turned to study her, wanting to take her hand again but feeling that friend-thing keeping him from doing so. "You know, I'd never considered it like that, but I think it's pretty accurate. I don't know if I'd call you a *flirt*, now that I've come to know you a little, but I do enjoy your company." Yes, he could say that much. It was true and also fit along her now-established boundary.

"I enjoy yours, too. And thank you for dinner. I had a great time."

"So did I."

At her door, she beamed at him, for all the world looking as if she had been given the biggest present in the universe. He wasn't sure what to say, but she took his hands as she had in the parking lot and pressed her cheek to his. "Thanks again. For everything. I'll see you at Easter Sunrise Service, okay?"

"Right." He had mentioned that he was preaching that one and she had said she wanted to be there. "I'll see you then."

"Goodnight."

He stayed on her front step until the door's lock was engaged and then took his time walking back to his car. Thinking, talking to God, trying to figure out what was going on here. Based strictly on body language—with which he was fairly familiar in general—Shelley was not pushing him away. On the contrary, he felt she was open. To him? To . . . something? He wasn't sure, but he had that sense from her.

But her words said something else, he thought. Not the greatest success with women, obviously, he still tended to believe a woman when she spoke. By her words, Shelley was playful, fun, adventurous, someone who wanted to improve her relationship with the Lord and do a better job serving him. On the other hand, she had *not* wanted to ask him out and she had clearly said she hoped they were friends.

Friends.

"So, is that my answer, Lord? *Let's be friends?*" He made some sound undefined even to himself as he reached the condos and his own home. "Dawn said to hang onto her, but you know best. I want nothing for myself that *you* do not want for me."

He said the words and meant them in his mind—but his heart rebelled.

"Well," he mused aloud, still in that mindset of prayer that he maintained most of the time when he was thinking things through, of whatever nature, "I'll see her on Easter. And if we're friends, then, Lord God, that will be fine. We'll keep in touch, she'll let me know when her VBS stuff comes in, and so on. I can handle that."

He even believed he meant it.

Seven

"So I would pray . . . your man will be God's man."

"Thanks, Dad, for letting me play in your shop. I *so* appreciate it." Shelley slid her goggles back down and turned again to her project. Her father had a complete workshop in the garage and she availed herself of it on those rare occasions when she needed to do some woodworking.

He eyed the book on the worktable while she was bent over the table saw. "You're doing what with this?"

"Making a plaque designed like that book cover. For his wall in his office."

"Whose wall?"

The screaming of the saw delayed further discussion, Shelley knew, but didn't entirely halt it. She kept the red oak plank level and guided it carefully through the saw. Losing half a finger was not something that appealed to her, so total concentration was necessary. Once that was done, though, she slid the protective gear off her face. *Might as well get it over with.*

"All right, it's Mark's wall. He's Dr. Mark Countryman. He's an associate pastor at that church where I was doing those calls. We've been to the beach, out to lunch, out to dinner, and he gave me that book to help me get started doing a better job of teaching the kids at church for Vacation Bible School. Have I missed anything?"

Her father stood there, lips twitching against a smile as the overhead light made his head shine. "Yes. What's the occasion with the plaque here, and are you really spending Easter morning with him?"

A tad uncomfortable, but also excited about the prospect of hearing Mark preach, Shelley nodded and held her father's gaze. "I am, yes. He invited me, since he's preaching at their sunrise service, and our church doesn't have one of those. And then he said there was a buffet breakfast for everyone and asked if I'd like to stick around for that. I would. If we're still friends by that time," she added, working the design into the template before setting up the computerized carving tool to copy it on the newly sawn plank. "I'll probably join him when Pastor Keller preaches. He's got a terrific voice, by the way, and I'm sure it'll be a good sermon."

"And the plaque? You don't usually make stuff for just anyone, I know."

"Well. In addition to it being Easter on Sunday, I found out it's his birthday. The Children's Minister at his church had it on her desk calendar. I thought it'd be a nice gift, you know? I mean . . . I can't give him one of my throws, right?"

Laughing, her father agreed that was perhaps not the best choice, given the time of year. "All right. Well. We'll expect you for an early dinner then, Shell. And your pastor? He's welcome to join us, if you'd like."

"We, um, hadn't talked about anything else, so I can't really say, but I'll be there." A man that fit all the things her mother had written about was wonderful, but family was forever.

Ear and eye protection in place, she started the carving tool and watched in careful wonder as Mark's book cover was etched into the piece of wood. She wasn't planning anything too fancy. Just the carving, beveling the edges with a rotary tool, signing it on the back, and letting a good sealing coat dry over the next couple of days. Then, she planned on gift wrapping it and leaving it on his desk. Given the opportunity.

It had been a long time since she'd had a friend to do things for. She liked her co-workers and all, but she really had left all her friends up in South Carolina. Friends that she had known as a little girl, friends who had known her mom and remembered how things used to be. She hadn't known Mark long at all, but she just felt that her mother would have liked him. And he had said they could be friends.

Friday and Saturday passed quickly. She eyed Mark's number on her cell phone a few times, but restrained herself. *No.* She was *not* going to call him. *No.*

Sunrise service was supposed to start at half past six. This was something of a logistical challenge. Dressing in a white linen skirt with a flared hem and a knit top with a ribbon threaded through the embroidered neckline, she felt she looked—suitable. Yes. Presentable, considering she was going to be sitting with the Associate Pastor during worship. She also brought one of her crocheted throws, just in case it was too chilly for comfort during the early service out of doors.

Bible and birthday gift in the passenger seat of her car, she headed to Mark's church. There was a big, grassy, park-like area to one side of the church and a sound system was in evidence, as was a low dais-like platform. Some musicians were there, and families and individuals were gradually filling the white folding chairs that arced toward the speaking platform. *How exciting!* The sun was not quite peeking over the palm trees to the east, but she knew it would be soon. *A glorious time and place to worship.*

Crossing the dew-damp grass, she was met by someone she recognized but who did not, at first, recognize her. "Good morning," the gentleman said, hand prepared to shake hers. "Welcome to our sunrise service."

"Good morning, Pastor Keller," she returned with a grin. He'd figure it out in a second.

He did, eyes widening with a smile. "Ah, yes, Jacob Cairns's favorite furniture technician. Welcome." He beckoned to a petite woman with a layered sort of bob cut on dark brown hair. "Annie. This is Shelley Roberts, visiting with us today. She was working on the furniture that Jacob bought for us."

Annie Keller offered her a warm smile. "Good morning. Ben told me about you. Said you had him laughing for two hours. Would you like to sit with us this morning? There's plenty of room."

Taken aback, she nodded. "Thank you. That's so kind of you."

Annie Keller took her arm companionably. "I'll get her settled, Ben."

While listening to what Annie had to say about her husband's version of her repair visit, Shelley was keeping an eye out for Mark. He was the preacher for this service, though, so she understood he might not be out and about just yet.

"Do you know where I might put this birthday present for Mark Countryman?" Shelley asked just before she seated herself. "So the gift wrap doesn't get damp?"

"Oh, certainly. Come. We'll go put it inside. Here, why don't you leave your, ah, shawl, here and then we'll be sure to still have seats when we come out. So, you got him a birthday present?" Annie Keller was all avid interest.

Shelley smiled a little. "Made him one, actually. Hope he likes it."

"Looks too small to be a bookcase," Annie teased. "Here, we can put it on his secretary's desk if his office door is closed." She met Shelley's eyes. "It is a little trying for the family and friends of anyone giving a sermon on a Sunday, let me tell you from experience. Ben will probably eat a quick breakfast with us this morning and then disappear into his office. Oh, look, the door's open."

Shelley heard the familiar voice as she approached. "Hello, Annie. Good morning."

"Brought you a present, Mark," Annie called, ushering Shelley into the office. "She'll be with Ben and me this morning. I'll, ah, see you back out there, Shelley."

Feeling a little breathless from the information, manner, and unspoken assumptions she had gleaned during her short walk with Annie Keller, Shelley was only able to smile a little helplessly at Mark, who was standing near his window. His suit jacket was over one arm and he looked about ready to step out and join everyone. "Good morning, Mark!"

"Shelley. Good to see you." His expression preoccupied, he crossed his office and took her hand, holding it a few moments before he noted the gift wrap. "What's that?"

"Your birthday present! Here."

Obviously surprised, he accepted the simply-wrapped rectangle in its masculine paper and brown satin bow. "How'd you know?"

"I do have eyes," she reminded him, lifting her brow. "You don't have to open it now, if you don't want. I know you've got to get ready for your sermon." It was so nice just to look at him, she was thinking. Just to breathe him in and see him and hear his voice.

He smiled. She melted just a little. It was the dimple-smile. Got her every time. "I do, but I'll be curious all morning if I don't open it." So he did, unwrapping the ribbon and carefully working the tape loose.

"You're one of *those* people," she remarked with a playful sigh. "Bet you can still reuse gift wrap, too."

"Never tried," he admitted, peeling back the tissue paper around the plaque. Then, "Oh. Wow. Shelley." He shot her a quick, disbelieving look. Setting the wrapping stuff on his desk, he held the gleaming oak plaque up to study it. "It's perfect. I've never seen anything like it before."

"Me, either. And thank you. I tried."

"You made it, right?" He turned it over to see her initials burnt into the wood on the back, with a small *Happy Birthday* along the bottom and the nail-space drilled in the top, so he could hang it up if he wanted.

She shrugged, not wanting to make an enormous deal out of it. It was, after all, Resurrection Sunday. "Well, I figured you probably weren't the crocheted blanket type, you know?"

He smiled, evidently distracted, but she knew she had done a good job and he was pleased in the way he looked at her. A depth of appreciation in the dark eyes and the set of his head told her enough. And that had been all she wanted. "So. I'll just go join Pastor and Mrs. Keller and see you after the service?"

"Of course. I'll find you. Maybe you could save me a seat at breakfast? It might take a while, come to think of it, before I can get there. Are you all right with that?"

"Sure. Whatever, it's all good."

"All right. And, wow. Thanks again. I really appreciate this. You must have worked really fast."

"You're welcome. See you later."

She left and meandered her way outside to find where her little throw was still on a chair with her Bible. Annie Keller was likely off greeting some other people as the seats filled up.

Before too long, the praise band was playing and a worship leader was singing and Shelley was on her feet singing, too. The songs were not that different than what she was used to and, when she was lost, she was able to follow the printed song-sheet Annie handed to her. The sun slowly worked its way up into the sky just before Mark took the platform and set his notes and Bible on a small lectern. "He is risen!" he said into the microphone.

"He is risen, indeed!" responded the worshipers in the traditional Easter greeting.

Shelley was unsurprised at Mark's command of his material, expected his presence to be strong, and was familiar enough with his voice. None of that threw her. What did knock her for an internal loop was how very *right* he seemed up there. A sense of purpose that said, *This is what I was made to do, and I am doing my best in the name of God.* She couldn't define it too deeply, but it moved her nevertheless.

After the sunrise service, there was a general mingling. Annie and Pastor Keller had their own Sunday morning duties to attend to, of course, as Senior Pastor and Spouse. *Now that's a job,* Shelley decided, gathering her things and watching Annie do the rounds. She caught Mark's eye as she left the general area and he crossed the grass quickly to her.

"That was—Well, words escape me," she told him, seeing him anew after hearing him preach. "Thank you so much for inviting me."

"I'm glad you were able to come." Seeing something over her shoulder, he turned and put his hand on her back to walk her back toward one of the church's outbuildings. "Breakfast is in the fellowship hall. You haven't seen it, right?"

"Not yet."

He seemed to be moving rather fast, but she imagined he—like Pastor Keller—still had duties this morning, so she didn't worry about it. She just tried to keep up as he settled her at a round table and placed his Bible on the seat next to hers. "I'll get back when I can."

"Thanks."

He hadn't taken three steps away when Shelley was surrounded. "Hello, dear. So good to see you," came a set of mature female voices from behind her. She rose to see who it was, and saw sharply dressed women, faces wreathed in eager smiles, approach with outstretched hands and words of welcome.

"You're the lovely girl who had lunch with Dr. Countryman," one of them said. "I remember seeing you two a week or so ago. Wasn't it?"

"At Bahama Breeze," inserted another.

"Oh," Shelley said on a breath, gathering her wits and composing her expression. "Good morning."

"So nice of you to share your Easter with us," another woman said. "Where do you go to church?"

"Good Shepherd Community? Over on—"

"Yes. Lovely little place. Good landscaper there."

Shelley had to smile at that. "They do take good care of the grounds, yes."

"Do you work locally, dear?" asked another lady who joined the group.

Shelley didn't have time to be disconcerted; she was just making sure she didn't embarrass Mark. "I do. I repair furniture."

That caught the cluster of women off guard, and Shelley appreciated the opportunity to breathe.

"So nice to have met you," one said before going off with her family.

Another one took her place. "What a lovely shawl. Where did you find it?"

"I crochet," Shelley said with a smile. *This is worse than a job interview.* "Do you?"

"Oh, my dear, not in years. Make shawls? Down here in *this* kind of weather?"

A bespectacled woman, with impeccable makeup, touched her arm lightly. "So where did you go to school?"

"I'm from South Carolina, actually."

And so it went, with questions about her work at her church. "Sunday School? Ah, lovely. Very suitable, too, what with Dr. Countryman being our Education Pastor." How long she had lived in the area, did she really work with furniture, and they *did* hope they would have the pleasure of seeing her again.

Over and over and over.

At length, she was rescued when someone interrupted the interrogation. "Shelley. I see you haven't been able to get your breakfast. Come along, we'll find you something before everything's cold, all right?" It was Kristi, the Children's Minister. "That is, of course, if you're planning on eating?"

"Yes, please." Relieved, Shelley was happy to be tugged along like luggage to the long set of tables where tempting aromas of fresh fruit, hot pastries, bacon, eggs and coffee reached out to the hungry.

Mark had emerged from the kitchens, after checking on details, to be greeted by quite a few folk on his way to some much wanted food. Accepting birthday greetings, too, from some of the people in the church who kept track of such things, and hearing not a few words of "Congratulations!" from others.

Thing was, what he wanted was to get back to Shelley. She was surrounded. He kept trying, though. He did. Waylaid as he was, he did believe he was making progress across the wide, table-crowded room. She was handling the attention well, he supposed, judging by the smile he could see and the smiles of the women around her. At last, though, Mark caught Kristi's eye.

"What is it?" she asked, reaching his side.

"Could you rescue Shelley?" he whispered over her head. "Mrs. Schuster . . ." Kristi nodded. "Thank you. Shelley's surrounded by meerkats." He regretted the word as soon as it slipped out—however apt it was, it wasn't kind to apply it to the honest and enthusiastic women of the

Naomi Circle—but a silent communication between himself and the young woman who was newest to the church's staff told him she'd never tell and, maybe, that she agreed with him.

Shelley did need rescuing. Friends they were, yes, he and Shelley. A friendship, perhaps, of a different kind for him, but he would do his best, and that included rescuing her. Even by proxy. Just seeing her this morning in his office had eased his heart considerably. And that gift she had made him.

He was still floored. How had she found out it was his birthday? She must have put some serious effort into it, too. There she was, working on that, and he was trying hard not to feel sorry for himself because she wanted to "be friends". If that was the kind of effort she brought to her friends, Mark decided as he finally made it to her side near the coffee pots at the end of the serving tables, then he should count himself blessed in her friendship, not sidelined.

"Hey, Shelley," he said. "Thanks, Kristi. I appreciate it."

"Not a problem, Mark. Have a good morning." Kristi left them with a knowing smile. Mark shook his head. *Women*.

"Sorry about that," he said to Shelley as he poured himself some coffee. "Did you get enough there? Anything I can try to find for you?"

She smiled and balanced her plate in one hand, her coffee in another. "I'm good, thanks. And sorry about what? It was nice of *Kristi* to come rescue me," she added with an arch look.

Chagrined, he hoped he wasn't blushing. "I really am sorry, Shelley. I had hoped that wouldn't happen."

They wove their way through the tables until they got to theirs, Mark all the while trying to get an understanding of how she felt about the inquisitive women. He was used to it, to a degree. It came with the job. Christina, up in Ohio, had understood it. Their break-up had to do with her ex-fiancé, not the "side-effects" of dating someone in the ministry.

Not that he and Shelley were *dating*. He just felt she had been put in an untenable position, without even asking for it.

Still, she smiled at him over the rim of her coffee cup. "They were all very friendly," she said, her tone polite. The smile, though, did not bring the lights to her eyes as it was prone to do when she was truly happy, giving him, at last, an understanding.

They would need to talk. Soon.

During their meal they were, of course, approached by several people who came to wish him a happy birthday, or a happy Easter. They also wished to be introduced to Shelley and, with each introduction, he winced internally. *This has to be driving her nuts.*

In between introductions and greetings, they managed to talk for a few moments. "Did you still, ah, want to stay to hear Ben?" he inquired hesitantly. Had she been completely scared off by all of this?

"Oh. Yes, I would. Thank you. I've been looking forward to it."

"What are your plans for after church?"

She shot him a quick, sharp glance. "My dad and his wife are planning an Easter dinner. I'll be over there. My brother has a game—Can you believe that? They play on Easter Sunday!—but he'll call us afterward. What about you?"

"Ben and Annie are having me over to join their family. Their kids come out and everything. It's a big dinner."

"Sounds nice."

"It is."

Something was lacking, though. Her usual energy and laughter weren't there. Mark prayed from his heart that no one had said anything to hurt or worry her. He remembered that she had said she could manage to hide it when she felt awkward. Was that what she was doing now? Pretending everything was all right?

It might work for the people who came to meet her, he reflected as they went in to worship a while later, but it didn't work for him. He knew her better than that, even in the short time they had been acquainted. He cared for her too much to be content when she so obviously was not. Still, it was good to sit in church with her. Was it just that she was someone? Anyone? Someone to share a smile with when Ben said something amusing? During the worship time and Ben's Easter sermon, Shelley lost that strained edge to her smiles. She relaxed, took notes, and exchanged understanding glances with him in all the right places.

When it was over and the congregation was shifting to make room for the next service to enter the worship center, he walked her to her car for that talk. He didn't want to let a problem sit and work until he could call her. Didn't want to talk about it on the phone, either.

"So?" He leaned on the low roof to her car, wondering how to ask. "Was it too much for one morning?"

She appeared flustered. That had to be a first. "Mark. Um. I hope I didn't do or say anything to embarrass you. I really do. I just—I just didn't know to be prepared for that, you know?"

He sighed, closed his eyes, and prayed that the Lord would give him the right words. "Maybe I should have warned you."

"Warned me? You mean, you *knew* that would happen?"

"Shelley, it kind of comes with the territory. I've been, ah, hearing from several sources how much they want to be introduced to my *lady friend*. I should have told you."

"But—I'm not. We're not—Um . . ." Frowning all over her face, she stuttered to a halt.

He took her free hand in one of his, thankful that she didn't pull away. "I know. Not sure what I can do about it now, but I know. And, again, I'm sorry. I never wanted you to feel uncomfortable."

She nodded, but then said, "I wanted to hear your study about James, too. But—But now I'm not sure if it's a good idea for me to come. I don't want to give anyone the wrong idea. It can't be helpful for you."

He hadn't even thought about that. "I told you before, no pressure. We're friends, right?" For him, it was very important to maintain that. Almost fiercely so. "I hope a group of well-meaning ladies isn't going to stop that."

He had hoped to coax a smile, a real one, and he did. "Yes, we are. I just hope I didn't cause you any further problems today."

"None at all, I'm sure," he told her with a definitive nod.

Still with her hand in his, she studied his face. He tried to keep it as open as possible, holding her gaze with his own while she processed whatever she felt was necessary. And when, finally, her lips curved into a smile and she stretched up a little to press her cheek to his, as she had before, he relaxed down his entire middle.

Her breath caressed his ear and he shivered. "Happy birthday, Mark."

He followed the bright yellow Mini Cooper with his eyes until it disappeared from view.

Eight

"I would pray that the man you marry is your friend."

Well. I'm forty.

If he had given the matter any thought at all twenty years before, Mark reflected the Monday after Easter, he probably would have said he would be married and have a couple kids by this time in his life. Patently, that had not been the case. Instead, he had a ThD, a condo in Florida, and a well-stocked kitchen.

This morning, lying in his bed with his fingers laced behind his head, he kept his mind in a state of openness to the Lord while he thought. The Bible said to *"pray unceasingly"*. He hadn't quite managed that, but he did try to keep his mind open to communication with the Almighty, figuring that the God who had made him and loved him, knew his innermost thoughts. Leaving them open to share and learn from was part of the relationship.

Forty. Alone. Still, he had to smile. Last night he had received birthday calls from his family. Two brothers and a sister and his parents. It had been heartwarming to visit with them. A lifetime of family love and camaraderie, inside jokes and shared memories. *Thanks, Lord, for them.* He prayed for the various concerns of his family and his friends, and that led him back to the remarkable birthday present he had received yesterday.

"What kind of wood?" his older brother, Matt, had asked last night.

Mark had held the gift in one hand and examined it again. "Haven't the foggiest. Kind of a rosy brownish shade, maybe?"

"You're dating a woodworker and you don't know what kind of wood she used? Didn't you even ask?"

"I was a little busy, remember?"

"I know. Just messin' with ya."

Brothers were great. Really. He hadn't felt it necessary to correct Matt's mistaken impression, though. It wasn't as if half the church, in addition to the *staff* at church, were operating under that same misassumption. Mark wasn't sure what to do about that. Dating the woman appealed to him.

He just didn't know if it was the right thing. She was so young. What—fourteen years younger, maybe? They had been comparing high school graduation experiences at some point while at Fort Myers Beach, so he thought that was about right. He had wondered, to himself, why he couldn't have met her ten years ago.

Because she would still have been in high school.

The youth minister that he had been for many years recoiled at the thought of dating one of those kids. Dawn's daughter, for example. Outstanding young girl, even as a freshman in high school. She was probably much like Shelley was now.

"Good grief. Lord, what am I *doing*?"

Giving yourself excuses. The notion occurred to him while he sat up in bed and reached for his Bible. *Time to focus.*

"Excuses?"

Excuses not to pursue her. Shelley Roberts is not, and has never been, in any of your ministries. At all. Not even close. She's not even a member of your church. What are you afraid of?

He tapped his Bible on his knee, thinking. Shelley had, as a matter of fact, turned down the idea of a date, yet seemed entirely jubilant about being his friend. Not in the way some women were "friends" with a man, either. But with a real smile and the eye-sparkling delight he had come to anticipate.

And, for that matter, he wanted that himself. There was something vibrant and life-affirming in just spending time with her. But she had indicated that the whole ministry-fishbowl thing was probably not a way of life she would be comfortable with, hadn't she?

Well. Being friends was a blessing, still. It was.

Doesn't mean you can't ask for more.

"Yes, it does. I'm *waiting*."

For what, gift wrap?

"Yes," he decided. "Something like that. God, I don't want to anticipate. I want to go alongside your will for me."

As he wrenched his mind and gut from the wishes and—he suspected—desires he had regarding Shelley, and her smiles and sheer joy in the moments of life, Mark buried himself in what was, of course, *her* favorite book of the Bible. The one from which he was teaching, beginning Wednesday night.

The lesson series that Shelley herself might not even attend, now that she had been interrogated so thoroughly. Frankly, he couldn't blame her.

He had studied this book, of course, but was reading it over again in preparation when something hit him. *James talks a lot about faith. We see him as a practical writer, Lord, but he uses the word "faith" a lot.*

Feeling kind of charged, he rose and found his laptop, pulling it out and starting it up. He did a quick check on a website regarding how often James used the word "faith" in his book. Sixteen times. For a book that was about being proactive, there was a lot there about just believing.

But "works" appeared thirteen times. Not an insignificant number.

For him, faith had been his bedrock for a long, long time. So, what was going on inside of his head at the moment? Was he going to sit and dwell on it, or do something about it?

That was not a hard question to answer. Not really.

> To: Shelley Roberts
> From: Mark Countryman
> Shelley,
>
> I wanted to thank you again for the plaque. I have not received a gift more perfectly suited to me since elementary school. Can't decide where to hang it, though! :-) What kind of wood did you use? My brother wanted to know and I couldn't tell him.
>
> It was a real pleasure to have you at worship services yesterday. I hope you and your family had a good dinner.
> So, it's Monday. Your day off and mine. I hope you get a chance to rest today. I'm actually thinking of going swimming.
>
> Remember, if you have any questions about that book at all, write or call. I know we still have a bartering arrangement and I don't want to let you down.
>
> Thank you again. You made yesterday very special for me.
>
> Mark

He read it twice, and then sent it. If she didn't answer by, say, Wednesday, he would probably figure that what he was now privately calling the *meerkat interrogation* had done more damage to their relationship—such as it was—than he had been able to heal in the short time he had had Sunday morning. He prayed it had not.

And he hoped she would answer sooner rather than later. His mind strayed often toward his computer over the next hour or so.

Cleaning the place, doing some laundry, taking a shower. Swimming. He had said he might do so later. When it warmed up a bit. The Weather Channel was predicting a high in the upper eighties today.

Unable to handle the suspense, he finally checked his e-mail.

> To: Mark Countryman
> From: Shelley Roberts

Mark -

Good morning!

Boy, you're up early, aren't you? :-) I'm so glad you liked your present. I enjoyed making it. The wood is red oak, so you can tell your brother.

Yes, a day off. I'm measuring my windows today, and doing some research about what kind of storm shutters I want. I have been using plywood, as I may have told you, but I really don't feel comfy in a dark house without any sunlight at all. So I'm looking into some different options. Have you started any hurricane preparations at all? You told your friends, you know, that you would. I'll help, if you want. No bartering needed. ;-)

Swimming . . . I enjoy swimming, but it's still not hot enough for me to brave a pool. I usually wait until mid-May or so. Let the water get warmed up. Maybe, though, your pool is heated? I hope you have a chance to relax. Yesterday had to be draining for you.

I had such a good time yesterday. I don't mean to gush, honest, but your sermon was great. I knew it would be—I've read your book—but sometimes . . . Sometimes, you know, someone is doing exactly what they're supposed to be doing and everything fits. Like my brother with a bat in his hands. You belong there.

Hope you have a great day,

~Shelley

    Yes, he admitted it. He had felt out-of-proportion happy to see her name in the inbox. Happiness had paled, though, next to a deep sense of heart-satisfaction when he read her letter. Yes, her sparkle was back. The good women of the Naomi Circle hadn't sent it away entirely. He was more than thankful.
    Encouraged, he wrote her again and they exchanged e-mails every day that week. Thursday evening, after she had not come to the Wednesday night Bible Study, he called her. No pressure, he assured her. He just wanted to know if she would like to have his text for the study. "Oh, wow. Yes, thank you, that would be great."
    He had listened in profound gratitude as she told him about her week. Enjoyed sharing with her what he could about his week, and they just talked. Talked until her cell phone needed charging.
    "Nope, never got a landline," she told him. "This works. Usually."

He did not ask to see her again, though. Not just yet. One thing at a time. He was not going to rush anything or see gift wrap where it wasn't.

It wasn't easy.

"Hi! Shelley Roberts, here for the cut and color." Inhaling deeply of the chemical scents to be found at the styling school's salon, Shelley relaxed within herself. There was something soothing about the black partitions. So clean, with the white and mirrored workstations. And all the hair stylists in their black shirts moving from station to station. She smiled.

"Ah, Courtney will take care of you today. She'll be ready in a few minutes, if you'd like to take a seat."

Shelley sat down, picked up a styling magazine, and absently flipped through the glossy, full-color pages. She wasn't seeing any of the sharp-boned models, though, or reading the articles about new hair color treatments. Her mind was dwelling on the month of April with a mixture of anticipation and dissatisfaction.

It had been a strange few weeks. Three weeks and a day, counting today, since she had seen Mark Countryman. *Three weeks.* Seemed impossible, but it was. Three weeks when they lived and worked—she had clocked it—less than ten miles from one another. She didn't understand it. He wrote to her every day. The guy wrote her an e-mail—often more than one—*every single day*. In her experience, men were not big on writing, so this was welcome. And he called her almost every day. They talked for hours every week—usually until one of their cell phones threatened to die. It was like being in a long distance relationship without the long distance. People did that, right?

And in all those words, spoken and written, she had listened and looked for the words asking her out. On a date. Something planned. Something right. Because, Mark being Mark, that's what he would do. He would take the time to think about it. To plan on the right thing to say, the right place to go. And then he would ask her. If it was a real date.

Hence the reason for her dissatisfaction. Was she not *date-able* for a minister? Yes, she had been flustered and unprepared for the worse-than-a-job-interview Easter Morning Breakfast Scene. Yes. She hadn't been warned, though, what to expect. She had seen, of course, how people acted with pastor's wives and all, but she wasn't, and he wasn't, and they weren't—

So she got over it. More or less. She still wasn't going back there again. Not. Just. Yet.

Replacing one unread magazine, she pulled out another one to blindly peruse its contents. Despite Mark's unfathomable behavior, she felt a little like a girl waiting for Christmas.

"Shelley Roberts? Courtney's ready for you."

Off to the right to the shiny black and white workstations, Shelley followed a girl with hair more blond than her own, with brown streaks tucked under the blond. It was unusual, but this was a styling school. The girl had the name Courtney on her lanyard, was slender of body and round of face, her lip pierced with a silver stud, and what looked like a tattoo around her wrist. Had to be permanent, Shelley guessed, with all the chemicals a hair stylist immersed their hands in all the time.

"Hi! So. You want to color your hair and get it cut? What do you want to do? Your hair's so pretty." Courtney met her eyes in the mirror, assessing, Shelley imagined, what was going to be happening.

Shelley shrugged. "Well. I'm wanting to go back to natural. I went all blond when I turned twenty-five last year, and this year I thought I'd try natural again. Just for a change. And I want the cut to be shorter. I think they called it *shattered*, or something, when I had it done last. I like it, I just want it shorter."

Courtney's narrow brown brows rose high into her pale forehead. "So, what's natural?"

With a laugh, Shelley had to shrug again. "I think it's light brown? Ish? Lighter than my eyebrows by a few shades."

"That'd be a big change. I would recommend that you go with a reverse frosting, in a dark blond tone, to make a gradual transition." The young stylist smiled to the mirror-image of themselves. "You don't want to shock anyone, do you?"

Shelley considered this for a moment, rolling her lower lip between her teeth. "Well. I have to tell you that yes, part of me would love to shock someone, but . . . I guess I better not. Whatever you said will work, I'm sure. You're the professional." Well, a professional-in-training, but Shelley figured the girl had more know-how than she did. This was her craft, and she knew what she was doing.

Mostly. "I'll go get one of my instructors, okay? Be right back."

Shelley enjoyed going to the school to get her hair done, because it was an education. Not just for herself, but also for the people who did her hair. Of course, the lower costs were great, too. Never had a serious mishap for the lower prices, either. The big drawback to coming to the school was the *time* it took. The hair stylists were in school. She, Shelley, was a client but also a subject. And the teachers had to check the proficiency of each student.

She was glad she had a couple of hours left in the morning.

The instructor returned, brought some swatches, and recommended that Shelley "go with this lovely dark blond shade" for a reverse frosting. "Next time, we can go a little darker and then your hair will grow out in your natural color and blend in with what's on top. It'll be a nice transition for you."

"You're the professional," Shelley said again, submitting herself to

Courtney and her instructor.

"So you said it's your birthday?" the young hair stylist said to make conversation.

"Yep. Well, next week."

"Got any big plans?"

"Not yet, but I'm hoping," Shelley said, smiling at Courtney via the mirror.

Hoping, yes. She was hoping. Hopeful. Waiting. *Preparing.*

Life changes worked best, she had learned, with preparation. When her mother had been diagnosed with breast cancer the first time, Shelley had been only four years old. She didn't remember much. Mom got better and, for years, life had been normal. Until, when Mom was thirty-five years old, the cancer invaded again. They had only had a few months. Just after Mom's next birthday, actually. Such a sad party, but they had tried to make it positive. Mom didn't want them to mourn overmuch. "I don't know about the rest of you," she had joked weakly from her special in-house hospital-style bed, "but I'll be just fine."

The family had had time to prepare. Time to see to the details of things. To strengthen themselves against the suffering of a most beloved woman. To hold and cry and love and know, when the end came, that it was a merciful, peaceful thing to reach the end of a time of pain to enter an eternity in the arms of God.

Preparation had been key at other life changes, too. When Stevie had gone to college, Shelley had had time to prepare. When Dad moved them down to Florida, there had been time to say goodbye to everyone at home, time to ready herself. The job audition experience had not been something expected, but Shelley had had years of preparation for it, so she did fine. Buying her own home had been something she had worked and planned for as well.

Hurricane Cyrus, though, had been another story. She and Dad had not been prepared at all for that—Who had been that year?—and the week and a half without power, without so many things. Well, she and Dad had learned. Now, she prepared.

"All right, now that we've got your hair separated out, time for the color. What do you think?"

Shelley glanced at the small industrial bowls with the two different kinds of goop in them. "They look very, ah, *haircolorish.*"

Courtney laughed a little. "They do, don't they? But I think you'll be very happy with your hair when we're done."

Preparation for a change in her life. That's what Shelley felt was happening now. Oh, this minute, not so much, exactly, but the past few weeks had been filled with a delighted sort of bubble in her middle.

Something really great was going to happen. She just knew it. Every day, she prayed that she would be ready, too. Something to do with Mark the Unfathomable.

"You have a terrific smile," Courtney remarked, her gloved hands sifting through sections of hair. "Thinking about someone special?"

Shelley blinked. "How'd you know?"

The younger girl laughed lightly. "I see that expression a lot."

Color washing over her cheeks, Shelley continued to let her mind wander. Right now, she was in the mood to just *think*. Heaven knew she had the time while getting her hair done.

Mark was interested in her. She felt that in her middle. Was it just chemistry? That was part of it, for sure. Mom had said that the *zing* was important. But there was so much more. And it was like a roller coaster some days. Just hearing his voice made her melt. It was ridiculous.

She had stopped by the church last Wednesday on her route to leave him a note on his car's windshield. Laughed. Wondered what he would do. It wasn't much of a note. She just wanted to remind him she was close. That she missed him. Without actually using those words.

The next day, when she had come home from work, an envelope had been taped to her front door. There was a handwritten note inside, thanking her for *her* note and asking if her Vacation Bible School materials had come yet. Nothing earth-shattering, but he had gone out of his way to write, to drive out to her house, and leave it there during his work day. That was encouraging.

He was flirting, even by her own definition of the term. Even when they weren't spending time together, exactly, she felt that he was making the effort. So why hadn't he taken the next step?

Was he waiting for an excuse or something *else*? She was not going to ask him out. Didn't know if that was God's will for her or not, but she was still following her mother's advice. She hoped, she was preparing, but she was *not* going to ask a church's associate pastor out on a date.

She was willing to undergo more worse-than-a-job-interview moments. She was. If they came with Dr. Mark Countryman. Thing was, she didn't know if she had what it took to be the woman a pastor was dating. The bleached and highlighted hair, she figured, ought to go. She should maybe try to look more natural. Not that that was a Scripturally-based idea. More of a gut-call on her part.

It was probably stupid, but she was preparing anyway. Spending perhaps more time than usual on examining her own spiritual life, her own heart. Spending time even in this not-quite-a-long-distance-relationship with him, and being *friends*. Good friends and getting to be better friends. Maybe even *very* good friends. Someday. She hoped.

Finally, hair colored and cut into a multilayered, multi-shaded, short and sassy light brown, dark blond style, Shelley paid the front desk, left a tip for Courtney, and headed for China Town. She was in the mood for Chinese. And, since it wasn't Wednesday, Mark shouldn't be there anyway.

I'm waiting, she reminded herself with a smile. *Waiting*.

Behind the counter, the stylist at the register reflected to herself that that woman who had just left looked like she was ready for some action. She grinned. "You go, girl."

Nine

"My very best earthly companion."

"Mark! Usual today? It's not your usual day." Anne laughed, her dark eyes glinting with humor.

"Yes, I think so, thanks."

"Okay."

Mark settled into one of the chairs and glanced around the small eat-in area of the restaurant. Smelled like sweet and sour sauce, he thought, and whatever it was they used on the sesame chicken lunch platter. Rapid Chinese—he didn't know the difference between the languages and dialects—prattled along behind the counter as he turned his attention, as he usually did, to the world outside the plate-glass windows. His gaze passed lightly over a woman with short hair—it was some sort of arty combination of light brown and dark blond—sitting across the small space behind a magazine.

She was wearing familiar sandals, though, with a bow on them that he thought he remembered. His heart thumped with enthusiasm in his chest and he had to grin. Was it her? He had waited this long to see her, he would wait another couple of minutes. However long it took for her to realize she was being stared at.

Because staring he *was*. At what he could see, anyway. The hair wasn't quite right, but he knew it anyway. The hands holding the magazine. The line of legs underneath a long, flowing skirt, but he had seen them in shorts, sprawled on his office floor when she had fallen into one of her famous Gravity Wells.

At length, the magazine slid down and *she* was staring at *him*. No other patrons were here, so it was just the two of them. He couldn't seem to breathe, just meeting her eyes. Ridiculous? Yes. Like something in a movie maybe. It seemed like forever, but it had been—

"Three weeks?"

Her voice reached him across the tile floor. Different than it had been these last weeks, close and in his ear. He nodded. "And a day," he added solemnly. What had he been thinking? Well, he had been *thinking*, which was the point. At least for him. "May I?"

She bit her lips together, as if suppressing a smile. "Of course."

Crossing the restaurant, he was oblivious to Anne and the cooks and the sounds of sizzling vegetables and pans on steel and the variety of aromas. Questing brown eyes, with a hint of humor, followed him.

"You look great," he told her. "You didn't tell me that you'd had your hair colored." It wasn't his business, maybe, but she had often told him about most of her activities. His hand twitched, wanting to touch her. He had *missed* her. Especially after that first Sunday after Easter, when he realized that he missed her beside him. And now, seeing her across a plastic-covered square table, he couldn't think of a thing to say to her beyond commenting on her hair? Inane. Still, he was curious, so he left the question out there.

"My hair? Well, no, I only got it done just before I came here." Her eyes challenged him to ask more, though. He knew that much.

So he did. "Any particular reason?"

A wash of color slid under her skin. "One or two."

She was really making this difficult on him. Normally a voluble person, Shelley must have a reason, Mark figured, for her brevity.

"Shelley, lunch is ready. Mark, lunch is—" Behind the counter, Anne stopped and broke into a long string of laughter. "Oh! I see, yes. *Very* nice."

After facing the repeated questions from the ladies at church, the wry references from Kristi and Ben in the office, and even the nudges from California and home, Mark was past being taken aback by other people making oblique allusions to him and Shelley. He rose to get both their lunches and decided he was going to pull a Shelley and go off to do something "touristy" on the spur of the moment. With a gesture, he indicated to her that she stay in her seat.

Strange, he mused, even as he exchanged far-too-amused looks with Anne of China Town, *for two people who have had so much to talk about over the past few weeks, we haven't a lot to say, have we?*

"Ready?" he called to Shelley when he was done.

Rising to her sandaled feet, she nodded. "Yes. Are we going somewhere?"

Something, just then, settled with a very cozy sort of pleasure in his middle. "Assuming you don't have anything perishable in your car."

"Not a thing," she assured him, eyes dancing.

Swinging one lunch in each of his hands, he smiled easily. "Then I'm driving. Come on."

Still with that expectant taciturnity between them, they left the restaurant and went past the cars parked next to the stores and out more to the middle of the lot. He saw the yellow Mini off to the right. "D'you need anything from your car?"

"Not just now, no. Thank you." Very proper, but he sensed laughter still lingered.

They were just reaching his car when he noticed the puddle from a morning rain shower near the right rear tire. "Careful," he advised.

Flashing him a look over her shoulder, she merely hopped. And when she landed, it was into a Gravity Well. "Whoop!"

"Shelley!" Hands full, he straddled the small puddle and scooped his arms under and around her to keep her from falling entirely. She was no lightweight, but he was equal—thankfully—to the task as she braced her hands on his shoulders. "Whoa," he murmured, the white plastic bags from China Town in his hands and a blushing woman in his arms. Her eyes were wide and fixated on him. Catching his breath, he managed to ask, "Are you all right?"

"Gravity Well. Never fails," she whispered.

He adjusted her more comfortably against himself and leaned against his car, relishing the weight of her body pressing into his. "I've found that out," he whispered back. He enjoyed having his arms wrapped around her, feeling the intimacy of heartbeats. There wasn't another sensation like it.

Her words was soft. "Oh, I'm so glad. I'd hate to have to do another demonstration for your benefit."

A hundred things suddenly leapt to his lips to say, to do, but he felt unequal to anything just then. Instead, he lowered his head and touched his forehead to hers as her breath caught audibly. "Do me a favor, if you would."

Her voice shivered out from somewhere near his chin. "Is it barterable?"

Leaning back, he had to smile. "I'll have to get a ledger and keep track, if it is."

At last, she grinned at him. "So, what's the favor, Dr. Countryman?" Her voice rang with mischief and he was entranced by her confidence and playfulness. "Need to know where you're taking me for lunch?"

"Olive Garden?"

She angled a look at one of the bags. "Too late."

"I know. Let's go." With incredible reluctance, he let her go and opened the passenger door to his car. She took the white plastic bags and balanced the food on her lap but before he could close the door, she looked up and squinted against the sunshine. "Mark?"

Crouching down, he was then able to alleviate the strain on her eyes and neck. "What?"

"At the risk of repeating *both* of ourselves, are you asking me out?"

"Yes."

He didn't understand her sudden laughter, but he was happy enough to hear it even as he closed her door.

Shelley was just drinking him in, giving thanks and laughing to herself. She had been so wrong. No formal *anything*. "Where are we going?

"Oh, about a mile."

Her heart was still pounding. From nothing to everything, almost, in the space of maybe five minutes. *Maybe*. From a long-distance-quasi-relationship to being in his arms and she hadn't been able to think of a thing to say to him.

Get a grip, girl. She tightened her hold on the handles of their lunches. "Oh! A picnic on the river. Excellent." So what if little bits of rain lingered in tiny puddles? So what? She had spent five weeks growing close to this man—something she knew she wanted more than just about anything—and here he was and he had surprised her. *Perfectly.*

There were sheltered picnic tables near the riverbank, next to a fenced-in area filled with small sailing craft. The beach with its white sand, edged with the green grass. The restaurant she had gone to with Mark to see his friends was right there, down The Walk. Fishermen cast their lines off the pier. It was warm and breezy, not too humid at all. She smiled into the winds as she and Mark settled themselves at a sheltered table, simultaneously deciding to sit on one of the concrete benches and face the river, while their lunches sat behind them in white Styrofoam boxes. Now that she was here with him, Shelley was not all that hungry.

Apparently, neither was he, for he didn't eat right away. He just popped open his can of ginger ale and sighed with pleasure. In the day? In his beverage of choice? She didn't know and didn't care. It was enough to see him. To see the somehow breath-stopping dimple at the corner of his mouth when he smiled at her.

"You know, for two people who have talked their phones into near spontaneous combustion," she remarked at last, after sipping her own soda, "we sure are quiet. Suppose we've run out of things to say?"

"Doubtful," he responded immediately. "Highly doubtful." He sipped again, still smiling. "Honestly, I'm just enjoying *being* with you. It's been a while."

"It has."

With a pensive air, he rolled the soda can between his hands. "May I ask you a question?"

"Of course."

She watched with tender amusement as he sifted through what he wanted to say. This, at least, she recognized. The sudden invitation had surprised and delighted her, but *this* was the Mark she knew and understood.

"It's all right that we're, ah, out? On an impromptu date, maybe, but out?"

Sheer relief and joy coursed through her. "Yes."

"But before," he said, watching her face now, not the green can still held between his hands, "you didn't seem so open to the idea. Even rejected it, you know? Did you have to get to know me first?"

"No. Not exactly. It's just that you were a customer, right? In a way. Besides, my mom told me I should never ask a guy out." She wondered what he would say to that.

"What?" He paused, studying her again and leaning toward her so that his elbow rested on the table at their backs. "I thought, pardon me, Shelley, but I thought your mother died when you were ten."

She looked away from him then, to contemplate the lapping waves of the river as it reached the beach. The tide was rising. "She did."

"Did she have this talk with you that young?" He sounded so genuinely perplexed that she rolled her head over to look at him and placed her soda can on the table.

"No."

"Then, how?"

Back to the river. Could she tell him? Of course she could. He was very nearly her best friend, wasn't he? She thought so. And he was a *pastor*, so this was not something that he would be unable to listen to, surely. "When Mom got sick, the second time, she knew that that was it. We all did. We tried," she continued, remembering and seeing the images of her mother's strained smile and her father's tears through her own, little girl eyes. "We tried. We went to school, did all the usual things. But while we were gone during the day, Mom wrote us letters. One for each of us, every year, for our birthdays. I have eleven of them." Her eyes burned, but she continued. "In each one, she told us what she thought was important. About life and God and family. All those little things, she told me, that she would have wanted me to know as I grew up." A smile tugged at her lips. "Including girl stuff. And boys. The letter she wrote for my sixteenth birthday involved dating. Even though it's old-fashioned, she told me, I should never ask a boy out. I tended to be too reckless and adventurous anyway, and if I waited, then at least the Lord would have a moment to curb my tendencies."

The wind dried the tears of memory from her cheeks as she drew in a slightly ragged breath. "I don't know what she wrote to Stevie. We never showed our letters to each other. They were very private."

She felt his hand encompass hers but didn't look at him just now, wanting to get a firmer control over her emotions. "So I never did," she added as a white, puffy cloud blew quickly overhead, casting a shadow on the sand.

"She must have been a remarkable woman, your mother," he said, his own voice unsteady, though his hand was not. "Your father, too."

"Yeah," she breathed. "Very. Dad raised us and didn't even look at another woman—I don't think—until he had given me that last letter on my twenty-first birthday. I think he felt then that he had done what Mom would have wanted him to do. Those letters—well, the first one, when I was eleven—were the reason I got saved."

His surprise washed over her. "Did your mother share her testimony in one?"

"Not really, no. But Dad, after I read the first one, told me that God's word is a little like my mother's letter. A letter from God to let me know he loves me. A letter to tell me what he thinks is important." She bit her lip before taking a deep, cleansing breath. "That really got to me. Dad said that at just the perfect moment—a God-thing, right?—and I realized, then, how much God loved me, too. And that was everything."

Mark was silent, but laced his fingers through hers comfortably. Comfortingly. Just letting her get herself back together. After a few minutes, he spoke quietly enough that she had to scoot over a little to hear him. "I didn't really internalize the relationship until I was twenty-one," he told her. "At a Christian college, believe it or not."

"What? You weren't born with a Bible in one hand, clinging to a pulpit?" she asked to tease him. It was his turn to gaze out over the river now, and she wondered what memories floated in front of him.

"No, not even close. I actually majored in history. My family were all Christians, and I was the one who rebelled."

"A *bad* boy?" she wondered aloud with a small smile.

Mark's laugh was short and flat. "Not quite. Met one of those, but I wasn't one, no. I just didn't get a sense of why it mattered, I guess. So, for me, it was a class at college. About the whole story of the Bible. How it's the Lord's story, from beginning to end, and it all has a purpose." His expression was tentative and maybe a little wary as he slid a glance to her. "I was overwhelmed. I had heard all the testimonies, I had seen God move in the lives of people, and I had been loved by a family who loved the Lord, but . . . for whatever reason, this hit me. And the next year, I felt called to go into the ministry." He squeezed her hand lightly before puffing out a big breath. "So."

"So?"

"You never answered my question earlier."

She blinked. "I didn't?"

"About your hair."

She flipped it with her free hand, accepting his change of subject. "Oh. Well. One of the reasons I got it colored was that I went all the way blond for my twenty-fifth birthday. Yeah, I know," she said to forestall any male-type remark, "it's probably silly, but I like to play, you know? This year, for my birthday, I figured I'd try going back to natural maybe. The stylist told me I should make it a slow transition so as not to shock anyone."

His laugh seemed to burst from his chest. "She doesn't know you very well, does she?"

"Nope. But it's all good. I like this."

"Me, too."

Pleasure burbled over her skin. "Really? Good."

He frowned. "Wait. When's your birthday?"

"Exactly one month to the day from yours."

Releasing her hand, he dug out his cell phone and instantly started pushing buttons.

"What're you doing?"

"Just a sec," he said, his cheekbones pushing into prominence while he changed screens on the small device. "Finding my calendar."

"Ohhh."

"I guess, with your birthday on a Tuesday, you can't just take the day off?"

"Can you believe I'm already booked? My dad and his wife are taking me to dinner that night."

"What about the Monday before?" he asked, now meeting her gaze with his own deep, dark one.

"What about it? I'm off, like you." She was going to *make* him ask.

"Do you have any plans that day, for your birthday?"

"Not yet . . ."

"Then, if it's all right with you, I'd like you to leave the day open. For me." She was on the verge of asking, but he caught her with a laugh as he snapped his phone shut. "And yes, I'm asking you out."

"Well then. I better go."

"Go?" He appeared a little troubled. "But—"

"I'm looking forward to it. But if I am going to do that, there's stuff I have to do today so I won't have to do it next week. Want to come?"

"Wouldn't miss it," he assured her. "Think this is still edible?" he asked, jerking his thumb at the white containers behind them.

She had forgotten her lunch. "Excellent. And yes, I'm sure it is. If not, we can maybe warm them up at my house?"

"Mine's closer," he said, sweeping an arm in the direction of The Walk. Right. He lived there, didn't he?

"Then let's go!" When he held out his hand to her, she took it.

Ten

"Oh, the time I had!"

"You absolutely have to tell me if I need a change of shoes or sunscreen or something, Mark," Shelley demanded the following Monday, standing hipshot in her living room. Barefoot. On purpose. She didn't want him hijacking her someplace until she had her answers. "I don't like going someplace without preparation. Last time, if you recall, I got a sunburn."

To give him credit, he nodded. "That wasn't my fault," he reminded her. Correctly. Then, he said, "All right. Let me think." He cocked his head and eyed her outfit, from the flared bottom of the light denim skirt to her sleeveless red top with the bows on the shoulders. "Sunscreen, yes. And you should have flats, I guess. No heels. Just in case." He grinned at her and she melted. Did he know he could do that to her? "Gravity, you know."

"Of course." It had been a week since the last time they had seen each other, but she would always remember that the last Gravity Well had landed her in his arms. "All right. Flats and sunscreen. Anything else?"

"Can you trust me enough to believe I've tried to take care of everything?"

She took a deep breath and stepped forward to close the distance between them on the Berber carpet of her living room. "You're my friend, Mark. Of course I trust you." She didn't understand the unusual line that furrowed between his eyebrows. "I'll go get my shoes. Be right back."

She heard him prowling around, checking out her books and opening her refrigerator door. "Checking on my food preferences?" she called from her room, where she was sliding on a pair of shiny red sandals—flat, of course—to go with her usual red purse. A quick check in the mirror had her freshening her lip gloss and checking to make sure her seams on her skirt and top lined up. All right. Picking up her sunscreen towelettes, she popped them in her purse and turned off the lights.

He was leaning against the strip of dividing wall between the kitchen and living room. "Nice place, by the way. I like the painting in the kitchen."

"Ah. Stephanie, my dad's wife, is wonderful with that kind of thing. She and my dad are so well-suited." *Welcome her*, her mom had said. Shelley had done her best.

"That's your memory smile," Mark commented as she checked to make sure all her doors were locked and her lights were turned off.

Color flooded to her face. She felt exposed. "My what?"

He hesitated, but repeated himself. "Your memory smile. The one you have when you're remembering something from your childhood."

"You make it sound all categorized and everything." Well, he was a man who liked things to be done in order, generally . . .

"I've offended you. I'm sorry. I didn't mean to."

She brushed it off. "Of course you didn't. I know you well enough to know *that*. Are we ready?"

"Are you?"

"Definitely."

Breakfast was at a restaurant at the Bell Tower Shopping Center. "This is a nice place," she remarked.

"I had heard it was." His smile told her that he had been doing some kind of research for today—she figured he had, by what she had gleaned during their conversations during the week—which made her grin.

The hostess appeared with big, leatherette menus. "How many this morning?"

"Just two."

"Right this way," the college-aged girl invited, walking ahead of them to the rear room of the place.

Once they had both ordered coffee and were left to themselves again, Shelley had to ask, "So, did you tell anyone about this?" she asked, gesturing between them. "Anyone give you a hard time?"

"Not too bad," he finally told her with a shrug. "You've been missed though. I can tell you that."

She felt the heat in her face again. "I'm sorry."

He brushed the back of her hand with his own. "Nothing to apologize for. Just wanted you to be prepared." His look was warm, and she felt it down to her toes.

"Prepared for what?"

"In case you ever decide to come to the rest of the Bible study or—or something."

Imagination supplied enough scenarios for her and she drew her lower lip between her teeth, thinking. "I'll have to think about that, all right?"

For a moment, he appeared somber. "All right."

She didn't want him to feel that way, though, when he was taking her out for her birthday. "What are we doing today? I'm absolutely going crazy wondering. Couldn't sleep last night."

He chuckled as their coffee was delivered to their table. They ordered and he leaned back in the booth, the low overhead lighting suiting the humor in his eye. He was casual today, wearing shorts—in her opinion, a must for comfort if one was going to be outside in May in Florida—and a neutral linen button-down with a subtle, woven pattern. Casual, but good. She liked that. She tried not to stare at the hollow of his throat visible at his open collar. It was one of those . . . *things* for her, she guessed. Hot button? Something? Sexy, anyway. Flushing, she glanced away, to the half-and-half containers. Opened one for her coffee.

He drank his black. Of course. "I knew you would," she murmured.

"Would what?"

"Drink your coffee black. So . . . What are we doing today?"

"Well, I had this idea." He checked his watch. "For taking a little trip."

Giddy. I think I'm giddy. Yes, this is how people feel when they use that word. "Trip? Us? Where?"

"Naples," he said, drawing the word out. Her giddiness ebbed away, but she kept the smile on her face. She practically lived in Naples, for work. Down there every couple of days. But then, he surprised her. "A water tour. I made reservations. A tour of the bay, really, maybe see some dolphins or manatee, and I've got a picnic for the beach."

Her pleasure washed back in full force. "Excellent. I've never been on one of those. It's perfect, Mark." Then, she had to laugh softly. "And so *touristy* of you."

He grinned and leaned forward. "I've had an excellent tour guide to learn from."

She felt kind of silly, during the rest of breakfast. A little lightheaded. They were talking, unsurprisingly, of birthdays. His, because of the wild stuff his family used to do to celebrate, and hers, because after her tenth, each birthday's greatest gift was the letter from her mother.

"They did *not* get you a car," she protested on a laugh.

"They did. I told you, I think, that I was a geek, right?"

"But debate team? You?"

"Me. And when I was chosen to be captain for the following year, my folks knew I'd need a car, so they . . . well, they bought me one."

"Nice to be some families. What was it?"

"A 1975 Datsun something or other. I just remember it was orange."

"Datsun?" The name didn't ring a bell.

He started, then a strange expression seemed to flow over his features like a waterfall before disappearing again. "Nissan? I guess maybe that was before your time," he commented with a wry note.

"I guess." For the first time, she had a strange impression: Mark was concerned, perhaps, about the difference in their ages.

She blinked. Should she address that? Tell him every man she had dated since moving to Florida had been at least ten years older than she? Or not worry about it, and hope she was wrong?

Well, it wasn't something to talk about here, anyway. It was her birthday date. She would hate to mess it up by making him uncomfortable. Another day. Perhaps he just needed to get used to her. In person, as opposed to on the phone or with e-mail.

"Ready for a boat ride?" he asked her later, when they had just about reached his car in the parking lot. "I was a little worried you'd already been on something like it, to be honest."

"Nope. It's going to be great." She turned to him on the walk and beamed. "You're the best. Really."

He ducked his head, looking for just a moment like a much younger man, before studying her from under his dark brows. "Best what?"

"Do you want a list?" she inquired playfully, continuing to walk backward so that she could watch his expression.

She saw it change, but not in time.

Had she missed the step? Tripped? Or just been a klutz? Didn't matter, because down she went. He lunged to try to reach her, but she had been just too far ahead, and she fell on the hand she tried to catch herself with, heavily enough so that pain shot through her arm. "Aiiii!"

"Shelley!" He was beside her in a moment. "Where? You hurt yourself, didn't you?"

"Mm." Biting her lip against a shriek of sudden, renewed pain, she closed her eyes. She felt the restless, worried motions of his hands on her ankles and even her legs. "Gravity Well?" she rasped, a hopeful lift to her brow.

He paused in his swift, cautious movements. She opened her eyes to find his, deep with concern. "Not this time, Shell. Can you get up?"

Offering him the hand without the major *ouch* attached to it, she tried, but not very well. He still wound up tugging her most of the way. "I feel so stupid," she said, tears spilling over. Ridiculous.

He led her to a planter under the shade of a leafy tree and sat her down on the slight rise of it. "Let me take a look at you. I've seen you fall a few times now," he remarked, his voice forcefully light, she could tell, by the edge. "But I've never seen you cry because of it."

"I feel so stupid," she said again, letting her head fall against his shoulder.

"Let me see your arm."

She gave him both of them, flinching at the grinding-teeth sound he made. "What?"

"Shelley, you're already swelling up." It was her left wrist. She could feel it. He leaned back a little so she had to move her head and meet his concerned focus. "Let's get you to a doctor."

The sun shining happily on them felt wasted now. "A doctor? No! C'mon, Mark. This is just a—a sprain or something. Happens all the time. And you planned such a terrific day . . ."

His lips firmed. "What if you broke it?"

"Couldn't be."

With a lifted brow, he blew out a breath. "All right. We'll try." He tried to smile as he rose to his feet. "I would rather spend our day on the water than at Urgent Care, myself. Can you bend your wrist like this?"

"Dr. Countryman. Are you all right?"

Mark winced internally and brought Shelley forward. "Shannon. Hello. I didn't know this was the place you worked. I'm fine. This is Shelley Roberts. She had a little accident after breakfast this morning. I think she may have fractured her wrist." Shelley was giving him an *I don't believe this* look, and he felt a smile coming on in spite of himself. Shannon Ellis was a member of the church, naturally, and had attended his recent class on the book of James. She looked different now, dressed in the soft blue tones required as a uniform in Urgent Care. Glasses prominent on her nose, she smiled in concern lined with curious interest. She had heard, apparently, of Shelley Roberts. *Great.*

Shannon's tone was entirely maternal. "Oh, dear. Do you have insurance, hon?"

The paperwork necessities washed over him while he looked into the glass-walled waiting area with its television and Formica chairs. It was still rather early in the day, and the clean, antiseptic medical smell was strong in the building. A baby snuffled and an older man coughed while a young couple tried to entertain a toddler.

"Mark?"

Instantly, Shelley's was the only voice in the building. "Right here. What is it?"

Embarrassment and shame welled in her eyes. "Um. I need some help filling this out. Maybe you were right. I think I might have broken it."

He flicked a glance to Shannon, took the clipboard and pen, and wrapped his free arm around Shelley. "All right. Let's get you seated and I'll see what I can do." Her left wrist had continued to swell alarmingly.

"Can you move it yet?"

"No," she bit out, lowering herself slowly to a chair. "I'm so sorry."

He squeezed her against himself just a little, in hopeful reassurance, and dared to nuzzle her hair. "Shelley, where can I start?"

Panic seemed to flare from her features. Distress. "I—I need to fill these out," she whispered frantically. "And I don't know what's wrong and I should probably call my dad and let him know and what about my calls tomorrow? Even if everything's okay I'm not going to be lifting any bookcases tomorrow, right? And—"

Whoa. Where was his confident, assertive, and cheerful Shelley? Clipboard on his lap, he took her uninjured hand in both of his and waited until he had her attention. "Hey. It's going to be all right. I'll be your hands for you, if you'd like. Are you a lefty?"

She blinked. Calmed a little. "Uh, no. And thanks. Okay. Sure. Okay."

He didn't like her pallor, so he checked her forehead with one of his hands. And then her pulse.

She smiled weakly into his eyes. "Dr. Countryman?" she whispered. "Is there another set of letters following you around that I don't know about?"

Chuckling, he shook his head. "No. I'm just—just worried for you."

Her forehead wasn't clammy or anything, so that was something. Her pulse was slowing. Her teasing notwithstanding, he had been with people after a minor trauma before. "And your wrist," he reminded her, "isn't getting any easier to look at." He reviewed what he would need to know for those forms. "Shell?"

"Hmmm? I love it when you call me *Shell*."

"I'll try to remember that." Smiling and shaking his head—she was incredible, she really was—he tried again. "Some of this stuff is a little personal. Are you all right with that?"

She nodded. Didn't seem to even think about doing otherwise. "Of course. We're friends," she said, as if he needed the reminder.

He wondered if *that* was the reason she had said yes to an actual date. "All right. Ah. I'll need your middle name. At least I know your date of birth . . ." At length, he only had to hold the board at a quasi-convenient angle for her signature. "Now, relax. I'll take these up to Shannon and I'm sure you'll get taken care of quickly."

"Okay."

That turned out to be a wish rather than a fact, for a motorcycle injury wove in, blood dripping alarmingly from an unprotected arm. Blood, of course, had priority with everyone, until the ambulance came and took the unfortunate rider away.

Shelley leaned back so that her head was on the wall behind them. "I am so sorry," she told him for the tenth time. "I ruined your whole day. I know you did all that work and made those plans and I just was a goof and ruined it all."

He stroked the back of her good hand. Lightly. "Hey, I am still spending the day with you, right?"

The laugh she gave him was choked. "Some boat trip. And the picnic is shot. And I had so looked forward to today, too." She sighed, wincing as she held up her left arm and examined her wrist again, as if willing it to heal before her eyes. "So now what are we going to do?"

"You mentioned that you wanted to call your dad?"

Her arm dropped gently as she closed her eyes. "I think I should wait 'til I know what's wrong exactly." She reached for his hand with her good one, tucked her fingers between his, and sighed again. "Thank you. Sorry for being such a baby."

"You're hardly that."

A spark kicked up in her expression as she tilted her head to look at him. "No, but I bet you've thought I'm too young for you."

"What?" How had she figured that out and why was she even bringing it up here? Now? Still, he had to be honest. "The thought had crossed my mind. I was a youth pastor when you were in high school, you know."

"So? Not *my* youth pastor," she murmured, turning from him again and closing her eyes.

He had heard that before, in his internal conversations. Smiling, he concurred. "True enough. Good thing, too," he tagged on, mostly to himself.

"I generally—"

"Shelley Roberts?"

She bolted upright in her uncomfortable seat and winced as she rose. "That'd be me. Coming!"

Mark stood alongside her. "Shell? You all right or do you want some company?"

"Please?"

With a nod, he caught her good hand in his. "Here I am."

Eleven

"Your dad is my best friend."

"I wanted to meet your pastor-fellow, but this was not the meeting I was thinking," Steve Roberts, Sr., murmured over Shelley's head on the night before her twenty-sixth birthday.

Shelley, propped up with her bright yellow fiberglass cast on a pillow on the arm of her sofa, blinked a few times. "Sorry, Dad. I'd kinda had other ideas about the day m'self."

Mark emerged from the kitchen with Stephanie. "Here you go," he said, a glass and Shelley's prescription bottle in one hand, and a water bottle in the other.

Stephanie, behind him, was nonverbally indicating enormous approval. Shelley made herself smile even though she was in pain. She wanted her meds and she wanted them an hour ago. "Thank you," she told Mark. "I really do appreciate this."

He poured her water while her dad watched with a careful expression. When she had taken her meds, Dad nodded. "Now, I've talked to Dinah, and she'll let Ronnie know about the rest of this week."

Shelley sighed. "I hate missing a week of work." Her cast practically glowed with guilt. "And what'll I do when I get back, Mr. Warehouse Manager?"

Dad chuckled. "Well, I'm sure I'll think of something that'll do ya 'til you can get back in the van again."

Stephanie tossed a lustrous lock of hair over her shoulder. "And I can make you some dinners when you come over tomorrow—" Her expressive eyes widened. "Oh, right . . ." Smiling broadly at both Mark and Shelley, she changed her plans. "You're both invited, of course, Dr. Countryman. And Shelley, dear, I'll make you up some meals so you don't have to cook too much this week, okay?"

Shelley opened her mouth to protest when Mark spoke. "First, thank you, Mrs. Roberts—"

"Stephanie, please."

"Thank you. I'm Mark, okay? Actually, I had thought I'd take care of her dinners this week, if that's all right with you, Shell?"

"Hmm? Okay, whatever." Shelley was waiting for the prescription to take effect. "Thank you," she said belatedly, meeting everyone's eyes. "You're all so tall."

They all had a chuckle and sat down in one breath. Mark was next to her. "I was thinking that it's my fault she got hurt, so it's the least I can do."

Shelley waved off his blame-grabbing. Carefully. But before she could put words together, her dad laughed with way too much enthusiasm. "That can hardly be your fault, Doctor—um, Mark. Shelley's been finding her Gravity Wells since before she knew what gravity was."

"Thanks a lot," Shelley muttered.

Stephanie chuckled, too. "We'll work something out, I'm sure, Mark. Are you going to eat what I brought for you tonight, Shell?"

"Hmm? What was it again?"

"Chinese take-out? From that place you like?"

Shelley found Mark's eyes and they both laughed. Steve and Stephanie looked on in considerable satisfaction.

After they had eaten, Dad crouched down next to her in front of her sofa while Mark and Stephanie were in the kitchen, washing up from dinner. "Shell, you gonna be all right here?"

Loopy now, her brain felt like it was floating somewhere on the Caloosahatchee. "I'm fine, Daddy. No problems. Feel just fine."

"Well. I guess he's okay. Beats that other man."

"Gucci-Man."

"Yeah, beats him by a mile."

"Thanks," she said, blinking a lot. "So are you guys going to go and let me tell him goodnight?"

Dad pressed a kiss to her forehead and rose to his full height, knees popping as he went. "Yeah. We will. You just take care now, okay? Call me if you need anything. I'll come by in the morning, make sure you're okay."

"All right, Daddy. Thanks."

"Stephanie? Ready to go?"

"Yes, honey. Just making sure Shelley has milk and whatever for breakfast tomorrow." Stephanie reappeared, her smile far too broad. "See you tomorrow night, you two. Shelley, get some rest, all right? The bookcases and bed frames of the Gulf Coast will survive without you for a week."

"Thanks, Steph. Will do. Thanks again for dinner," Shelley said. She wasn't going to try to rise to see them to the door. Mark did that for her.

"Alone at last," she quipped, relaxing more deeply against the pillows of her sofa. It was a high-end piece that she had picked up for next to nothing at a clearance event at the warehouse. She had rebuilt the frame and reupholstered the back panel and—*presto!*—she had a five thousand dollar sofa. For nothing but some sweat and spare parts, really. It was quite cozy to snuggle into, especially tonight.

The air conditioner kicked on as Mark sat gingerly next to her. "I was serious, you know, Shelley."

She tried to make her mind find what he was referring to, but it wasn't easy. "Serious?"

"Yes, about making sure you had dinner and everything this week. You know the church isn't far at all, and I can be here in less than ten minutes if you need me, okay?"

"Sure, Mark. Whatever you say," she murmured. "It's really bright in here, you know?"

His chuckle seemed far away. "Maybe I better write this down."

"Good idea. Write it down. Want to watch a movie?"

"Did you want to watch something?"

"You pick. I don't care," she said. "This is a serious painkiller."

"Uh-huh. That's what I thought. All right." She noticed only that he rose from the sofa and put in a DVD, bringing her the long, rectangular remote. "Here you go. I'll just go make some notes for you, in case you need them, all right?"

"All right. Thank you."

The light from the kitchen was the only one in the room by the time she saw the opening scenes to *Kate and Leopold*. Why that movie? She didn't know, but she thought that Mark Countryman was a very handy man to have around. Even if he didn't know a thing about hurricane shutters.

"Will that be okay with you, Shell?" Mark called from the small square dining table outside the kitchen. Light from the ceiling fan provided him with enough illumination to make a list for her, so that her eyes weren't bothered. Hey, if the lady said it was too bright, it was too bright, right?

No answer.

Smiling to himself at the notion that she was sleeping, he moved with quiet steps across the room to where the illumination from the television was lightly washing her face. Yes, she was out. Good. She had been getting a little goofy there, courtesy of her prescription. Good stuff, but it knocked some folks off their feet.

Should I leave her here or try to get her to her room?

Best to leave her. He did what he could to ease her current position so she would sleep with some comfort, as long as her wrist and cast would let her. That thing would smack her a good one on the forehead if she was restless.

He could manage to stay awake and watch over her, he supposed. *Just to make sure she's all right tonight.*

He decided he would. She was on medication and he felt responsible for getting her into this condition—whether or not that was entirely rational was irrelevant. Granted, he'd have to try to keep it quiet. Not that he was ashamed of her or anything—far from it—but so many people at the church had the two of them halfway to the altar by now, that even if he clarified he was acting in her best interests, it would not be well-received. No. Sure, he and Shelley were *friends*, but not in the eyes of a good portion of the congregation.

Moving the coffee table, piling pillows and getting all breakables out of the way, Mark felt he had done what he could to make sure she wouldn't inadvertently hurt herself with a sudden movement. Then he rummaged in her kitchen for some coffee. Even instant would do the job. He could watch a movie with subtitles, right? Or read a book. He didn't want to invade her space. Shelley could not take exception to his having done that much.

"So, has it been okay that Shelley doesn't go to your church?" Stephanie Roberts had asked him while they cleared up after dinner. "I mean, no one's given you any grief?"

"Over that? No. It's actually a little easier to be, uh, seeing someone not in the congregation."

Shelley's stepmother had paused in rinsing leftover rice and soy sauce into the sink, her eyes very sharply focused on him. "And you speak from experience, I'd guess?"

He met her gaze and nodded. "Yep."

She had dropped the topic and proceeded to point out where everything was in Shelley's kitchen. "Just in case, you know, you need to find her anything."

He used that information now as he retrieved items from her cupboards.

She had a kettle on the stove, so he heated water and spooned some instant coffee into a cup. He had to smile to see all the flavored creamers and things she had. He finished off his coffee quickly and returned to the living room and the place he had staked out for himself next to the sofa, inhaling deeply and preparing himself for a long night.

"Mark?"

"I'm here."

Her voice was slurred and she didn't even open an eye. "Good. Sorry 'bout today."

He cupped her cheek with his palm and smiled down at her. "No more apologies, Shell. Go to sleep. I'm going to be right over here, watching TV, if you need anything."

Her eyes fluttered open, surprise drawing her brows together. "Okay . . . Thangsss . . ."

Using the remote, he turned off the television and DVD player. It was dark, except for the kitchen light that spilled across the dining table.

"Lord," he prayed softly, "thank you. Thank you for giving us this day together. For letting her injury be relatively minor. Thank you for her family and their support. And thank you, Lord, for letting me be of what help I could. It's been a good day. It really has. Please let her body heal quickly and let her mind be fully occupied." He smiled down at her from his perch on the now-vacant arm of her sofa. "She's something else."

He left the kitchen light on. It apparently didn't bother her while she slept and when she woke, she might want the light. Double-checking the living room to make sure it was as clutter-free as he could make it, he checked again on her.

"Good night, Shelley," he whispered, brushing her forehead with his lips. He'd been wanting to do that all day, and saw no point in denying himself that pleasure now.

It felt sweetly intimate, being in her house in the near-dark while she was sleeping in the living room. He found the front bathroom, washed up, and tried to figure out what to do about staying awake if the coffee didn't work.

He moved around as quietly as possible, realizing he was wiped out. It was fairly early in the evening, but it had been a busy day, and he had expended a great deal of energy since waking up with the sun. Had it been only one day?

Not wanting to risk awakening her in his own efforts to stay awake, he chose a book from her shelves. A biography of John Adams that he had read before. While he read, he listened to Shelley's breathing, wincing when she unconsciously made small moans that sounded painful to him. Was she in pain or were her dreams painful? Or was she just someone who made noise in her sleep?

He couldn't let himself fall asleep. As tired as he was, he didn't dare relax entirely. He kept seeing her as she'd been earlier, with tears in her eyes or that thin smile on her face that she showed through the serious pain she had experienced. He had been there throughout everything that day, and it hadn't been easy on either of them. It wasn't a major catastrophe, and he had managed—he believed—to act properly and for her best interests. All while kicking himself for taking her anywhere. If they had had breakfast at, say, her house, this wouldn't have happened. He could have cooked for her. Then she wouldn't have fallen and been injured.

Now, give yourself some slack, he told himself. Like her father said, this isn't the first time this has happened.

Not with a broken bone.

Not your fault, he heard in his head again.

He was engrossed with sifting through the impressions of the day. The joy he had had in the morning, the fear—irrational, perhaps, but real—when she had fallen, his concern when her wrist started swelling so fast, and how he had just ached all over to see her tears. It had been like a kick in the gut, especially in the Urgent Care facility. Shelley had come unglued there, for a moment. And during the x-ray and setting procedures, she had gone so pale, biting her lip until it was bone-white. Every protective instinct he'd never known he had apart from the girls in his family had butted sharply against the knowledge that Shelley was more than capable of taking care of herself. She had needed a hand, not a bodyguard.

And one of her hands was now wrapped in that bright yellow cast. The color worked for her. So cheerful. So open and interesting.

"Mark, you really are the best," she had said with a sigh earlier, eyes unclouded before her medications kicked in, body relaxed in the long skirt and soft shirt she wore. *"I couldn't have made it through any of that without you."*

Still, he was ill at ease as he moved to stand near her feet. *I could go home. Get a few hours of sleep. Come back first thing in the morning in case she needs some help. I could do that.*

Then, three little words leapt to his lips. Three words he immediately suppressed, for they made no sense to him, then. It was too early, yet. He wasn't sure that this was The Girl, anyway.

The words made no sense to him now, but he whispered them into the quiet of the living room as he prepared to leave. "I love you."

He almost groaned in frustration, but stopped himself just in time. He whispered instead. "Oh, Lord God in Heaven, how is this happening? Why? I do not want what *you* do not want for me. You know that."

Frustrated, he turned and touched the doorknob. "What are you doing?" he asked himself in a raspy voice. "Lord, help me! She's too young, she wants nothing to do with being—being involved with me at church, and she keeps reminding me that we're *friends*. This is nuts."

The anger left him as quickly as it came and he checked one more time to make sure she was as comfortable as he could have made her. He ached, inside. Heartache. *I can live with heartache. I've done it before.*

Ah, the lights. He turned down the light he had used to read by and went to sit by her for a few moments, because the pull was just more than he wanted to resist. He settled down on the floor, clipping the coffee table with his elbow and wincing.

She moved a little. "Mark?"

Remorse speared him for awakening her, but he kept his voice low and soothing. "Right here, sweetheart. You're fine. You need your rest." The endearment had just tumbled from his tongue, but he didn't withdraw it.

"You, too. Why're you here?"

He saw her upper body shift, so he rose up to his knees. "Shh, shh. Lie back. Don't try to use that arm, Shell. I stayed just in case you needed me."

Her expression, though sleepy, relaxed in a smile. "Oh. Good. 'Kay. Sleeping?"

"Not right now."

Her laugh was uneven. "Well. Glad you stayed." She extended her good hand and he clasped it in his own, stretching a little way up her legs to do so. "Thanks."

"I was just going to go home, but I'll be back in the morning."

Her body jerked and he winced as she did. "Leave?" she murmured, her eyes open but seeming unfocused. "Stay? Please?"

She was so young. So vulnerable, it seemed to him. He held her work-callused hand in his own. She wanted to be friends. He had to remind himself of that. Her friendship was valuable, *invaluable,* and if that's all there was, he would wrap it around himself and be thankful.

"All right, I'll stay." She gripped his hand and he didn't have the heart to tug it from her, so he knelt on the floor between the sofa and the coffee table and tried to stay awake.

Mark, you really are the best, she had told him. Somehow, that would have to be enough.

Twelve

"God says that a man is not meant to live alone always."

"Oh, now I see, that makes perfect sense. I can do that." Shelley spoke rapidly over Mark's small dining table. "And then, I could probably do fewer over-the-top physical comedy things for the older kids, right? And have them read the Scriptures for themselves?"

The Vacation Bible School curriculum had come in and Shelley had, of course, availed herself of a published expert in Christian Education to help her prepare. Mark nodded, friendly but subdued. "You could do that, but," he added with a soft twinkle in his incredible dark eyes, "the older kids like the over-the-top stuff, too. Or you could get *them* to do it, depending upon how open you feel they are to drama."

"Oooh, that'd be fun," she mused, flipping over the pages to look for a supply listing. Were costumes there? "I could use costumes, right?"

"Even adults like dressing up," Mark informed her. "Want any more of that?" he asked with a nod at her lemonade.

"Oh, yes. I cannot believe you got the recipe for that lemonade, Mark, It's just perfect." She grinned at him, hoping to find that devastating dimple at the corner of his smile but, as had been the case since her accident, it was elusive.

He went to the kitchen, poured both of them another glass, and returned, but didn't sit down to drink his. Instead, he headed to his tiny lanai. Cute, functional, with just enough room for two small folding chairs and two standing adults. She joined him.

"Hey," she ventured, as they stood at the white wooden rails and gazed out at the river together. It was a quiet one tonight. Gentle. No stormy froth or high winds. The weather had been rather warm for mid-May. "What is it?"

He seemed distant. Again. It took him a couple of moments before he spoke. "What?"

"That's what I want to know." She tried a small, playful nudge with her shoulder against him. "Something's been bothering you. I feel like I should apologize, maybe," she confessed. "I know you planned so hard and everything, and I feel like every time you see this obnoxious yellow cast, you're reminded of how I blew it all by being an idiot. And then you stayed over . . ."

She blushed, remembering the morning after her fall. She had come out of her medication-induced slumber in a certain degree of pain, but before she moved she had had the presence of mind to do a mental inventory and had found—to her pleasure, to be sure—that Mark was with her, half-draped over her sofa, his fingers loosely entwined with hers.

He had awakened a moment later, looking embarrassed and disconcerted. *"I'm sorry,"* he'd stammered and then proceeded to slowly unfold himself to stand upright.

They hadn't really spoken about it since.

"What do you mean?" he asked now, his eyes hooded and not very communicative.

Her heart raced, heating the skin of her neck and face with a painful kind of embarrassment. "I feel like, like maybe you did something you felt was wrong, and it was my fault. And I messed up everything."

He shot her a sharp look. "No, Shelley. How can you think that? No. You weren't responsible for a thing." He cocked his head and might have smiled a little. "Except maybe walking backward. But no, Shell. I didn't do anything I felt was wrong." He looked at the yellow armor on her left arm. "How much longer?"

She sighed. "A month? Maybe. It's making me crazy."

Another ghost of a smile. "I bet."

Silence settled between them again. "We're still friends, right?"

He stiffened, then relaxed and sighed. "Of course."

"So, if it's not me or my cast, what is it? I don't know . . . I feel like it's my fault." She had begun with a bang, but ended with almost a whimper. She *did* feel as if it were her fault. As if she weren't enough or something. That ruined day two weeks ago had changed everything. "I know—I know I was kind of messed up, with the doctors and medications and everything. I guess it was . . . pretty weird . . . to see . . . I'm sorry if I did or said anything to upset you."

Sure that she had lowered herself somehow in his eyes, she could not bring herself to look at him. Instead, she pressed her head to the corner post of the tiny lanai and wished she knew what to say.

The lightest of light touches brushed the back of her neck, sending electric shivers over every inch of her body. She almost thought it was some small flying creature, but then it repeated itself in exactly the same way, and she sighed. Relief. Wonder. Curiosity. She had an overwhelming idea that she had to keep her mouth shut for a few minutes.

She tried.

Her near-empty lemonade glass disappeared from her hand, leaving cool wetness that she rubbed into her half-wrapped, half-exposed fingers. There was the faint sound of glass on wood, as Mark settled both their glasses behind them. Still Shelley kept quiet.

She heard him breathe deeply, in and out. As if he were calming himself, as she did before dealing with a particularly difficult customer. Was that how he saw her? A slice went through her middle at the idea. It smoothed away when he did the strangest thing. He wrapped one lean arm around her, just at the collarbone, and tugged her affectionately back against his chest. All without saying a word.

His thumb stroked her shoulder and she felt her mouth go dry. What was he doing? Did he even know? She had seen him every day for two weeks now. Every day. He had made her dinner that first week, every night. Every day he had spent time with her, to make sure she was doing well. He had helped her around the house with the vacuum and even mowed her lawn. The man was amazing. And a *genius* cook. Yet the whole time, he had held himself at this slight distance from her. A distance that hadn't been there even when she had ruined his carefully planned day. Aside from the most basic, "let me help you with that", he hadn't touched her. Not the barest fingertip.

"Have you ever asked the Lord why on earth he was allowing something to happen in your life?"

That Mark Countryman, ThD, had murmured such a question into her hair was disconcerting. Still, weren't they friends? In spite of everything? *Yes.* And friends should be able to talk about this kind of deep stuff as well as the lighter fare of living, right? This didn't sound, though, like it had anything to do with her, so Shelley breathed easier on her own behalf while hurting on his. He sounded like a man who was really seeking. Hard. And not finding.

"Yeah," she murmured, her own voice soft enough to carry only up to his ears. With unconscious motions, she stroked his forearm with her fingertips. "When my mom died."

"Ah." She felt, more than heard, his apology in the way his arm tightened for a moment. "That's a hard question to have to ask so young."

"A hard lesson to have to learn, too, but . . ." She smiled, wanting to encourage him, and looked up and around, craning her neck. She hit his chin with her cheekbone as she did so, and managed not to sigh at the wonderfully masculine texture of a whiskery chin. She really liked that. "I learned it."

"And what did ten-year-old Shelley learn?" he wondered, tilting his head closer to hers.

"I learned," she breathed, needing to answer but having this urgent wish to nudge her chin up that inch necessary to meet his lips with hers, "that the question should never be 'Why?' because we'll never understand. Sixteen years later, Mark, and I still don't understand."

Her heart was pounding like a crazy thing inside of her, but she held very, very still. His black eyes dove into hers. It was amazingly intimate. Eerily intense. "That's a lot for someone so young to learn."

Not one word. She couldn't find one. She wanted to, but she couldn't. She stared, sure that it was getting darker as they stood out here like this. Still, this was the best and only place she wanted to be. Right here. Right now. At last, she managed, "I'm still learning."

"Me, too," he said as he turned her slowly around, maintaining eye contact. "So, *why* is the wrong question," he continued, as if he were not making her crazy by holding her along the length of his body, her good arm around his shoulders while her dangerous one rested awkwardly in the crook of his elbow. "What's the right one?"

He *had* to know the answer. He really was a wise man, so she had to figure there was a reason he was asking her about this right now. She didn't know, but decided to keep going with this. He hadn't felt so close to her for weeks.

She relaxed a little more against him. "Well, I heard asking *why* is wrong. That instead, we should be asking *'What do I do now?'* or *'How do I respond?'* to whatever it was." Her fingers drifted into the dark curls of hair brushing his neck.

"Does that help?"

She smiled, sure now that he was teasing her, even though his expression remained solemn. "So far, it's been good advice."

"What if you're not sure what to do?"

Recommitting to following his train of thought to its caboose, she still had to look away. She was only human, and the magnetism in his questing gaze was beyond her ability to meet without her mind spinning. "You can only step forward, right? Try something. Pray. That's what I do anyway. And then," she added, smiling just a little before daring to look up at him again, "you just have to be brave, I guess."

He gathered her even closer than he had before, taking her breath away. "You're an inordinately brave person," he whispered, just before he lowered his lips to hers, inch by inch. As if giving her every chance to turn from him.

When she was sure that he wasn't going to make a sudden stop, she closed her eyes and leaned even more thoroughly into him, sighing as he took his time, tasting, luxuriating in something she had been wanting for months. *Yes! Yes, this is what I've needed . . .* Heat blossomed within her, and she relished it. His fingers gripped her, one hand sliding intimately through her hair.

"Shelley," he whispered as he moved to breathe.

Not thinking, just wanting *more*, she slid her other arm up around him, too.

That is, she tried. He winced and lifted his head right away, his whole face crinkled against the discomfort.

"Only me," she said, burning with embarrassment and ducking her head near his throat. "I'm sorry."

"Only you what?" he wondered.

"Only I would manage to ruin something so perfectly perfect with a neon-yellow cast."

"Perfectly perfect?" He sounded as if he were smiling.

She blushed in the darkness. "I'm only going to say it once."

Her heart still hadn't calmed down, but she took their lemonade glasses into his kitchen. "I, um, better go."

"Are you all right to drive?"

"Do you feel like you need to follow me home? Again?" He had done so once, last week, after a quick run to the grocery.

"I guess not," he said now. He stayed on the lanai until she had gathered her VBS materials and slid her sandals back on her feet. When her keys jingled, he re-entered his own home and shut the glass doors behind him. "I'll walk you out," he said, taking her hand.

Once out of doors, curriculum in front of her and purse over her shoulder, Shelley filled her lungs with the air of the Caloosahatchee. "Thanks again for your help," she said, as if he had only fulfilled his part of their long-established barter. "I can't tell you how much better I feel about facing the kids at VBS."

"All part of the service." At the driver's door to her Mini, he waited while she tossed her stuff in—the top was up, this evening—and turned again, the yellow steel door between them like a short but effective chaperone. "Thanks for your help, too," he said, ruffling her hair with a casual hand.

She blushed. "Um, okay." What did a girl say to that?

"When's your VBS start?" he asked.

"A month from today."

"Good." He kept her there with an air of expectation. "I was wondering . . ."

"What?"

"That James series is over this Wednesday. Do you want to come to the last class?"

"Well, I have been keeping up with what you've sent me and brought over," she said, wondering if she really did want to face all those people. But that was part of who Mark was, and so . . . "All right," she said slowly. "I'll be there."

The devastating dimple made an appearance at last, gladdening her heart. "I can't wait." And, flouting the short steel chaperone, he kissed her again.

"You just have to be brave, I guess." Mark kept Shelley's words tucked in

his heart over the next several weeks. Weeks in which he had tried to do as she had advised. For all his years and all his education, he guessed he lacked some very basic wisdom.

He had taken her advice, he felt, in kissing her that first time. Trying something. Moving forward. He had made sure to make it a kiss that would not in any way be a friend-to-friend kind of embrace. Not even close. And it hadn't been. *Not even close.* He kept the amazing, vivid sense-memory with him, near his most conscious thoughts. The way she had filled his arms. Whenever he let his mind return to that moment, just before her cast had interfered, he had to close his eyes and center himself.

Shelley had come to learn from him that evening, but she had been an effective teacher, too.

She was, indeed, a brave woman. Prepared, as she had said, she went to that last study on the book of James and had been predictably surrounded. That time, though, he had stayed at her side so that she wasn't nearly so overwhelmed. Sunday mornings, she had continued at her church, which didn't bother anyone, but she was with him in the evenings.

Not an easy thing, he knew, dating an associate pastor. Especially not with a neon-yellow cast attached to your arm.

Well, that was gone now. Removed the very day that Vacation Bible School had opened at her church.

Tonight was the fifth of July. He had been gone for a little more than a week on vacation. Visiting his family in California. Celebrating with them with the family's traditional picnic and home movie marathon. With an evening of "Do You Remember?" and watching fireworks on television. This year, for added family entertainment, he guessed, there was the question: *Where's Shelley?*

Shelley would have needed extensive prep time to get ready to meet his family. He hoped and prayed, sincerely, that it would be required. Eventually. But, after Shelley had been introduced via cell phone, all the way around, there was still another topic of conversation that had *not* been there before he had moved to Florida.

"It's hurricane season," his sister, Joanna, had said, pouncing on him like a college student instead of the thirty-something mother of three that she was. "Mom said that you had someone there to help you get ready this year. I am so glad, Mark. I get so worried!"

"Not you, too," Mark explained to each of his siblings that he had purchased supplies and some batteries. Water, a cooler, and batteries. That was *it*. He loved Shelley Roberts. He loved his family. But they were all, to borrow a Shelleyism, way over-the-top-paranoid about this whole hurricane thing.

Being brave had played no role in his vacation. It had, though, been excellent advice for his relationship with Shelley. Had she known what he was talking about that evening? He hadn't quite managed to ask her, not once in their various dinners, lunches by the river, or the occasional conventional movie date.

Being brave, as she had said, was just another way to say he was acting in faith. Just as he had known he had to, months ago. But he still felt something was missing. Was he blind, or was the Lord withholding something from him? The awareness of his ignorance kept him from declaring himself, he knew. Those "three little words" were very heavy when kept bound on a tongue.

The flight from California landed smoothly, but Mark felt his heart jump.

"I'll wait for you in the cell phone lot," Shelley had told him. "So, call me when you land."

Late as it was here, he knew she'd be there. Alone. He did worry about her, of course, but said, "You be safe out there. Bring a bat or some pepper spray, will you?"

She had only laughed. "So long as I don't try to actually walk to the gate, I'll probably be fine."

They figured out where he should wait for her—there were so many doors and landmarks to choose from—and, before he thought it would be possible, there was the familiar yellow Mini, top down. And a *brunette* behind the wheel.

"You got your hair done again?"

"Oh, and a lovely hello to you, too, Mark. Get in!" The brilliant smile on her face told him he was forgiven. After tossing his luggage behind the passenger seat, he slid into the car himself, happy to be home.

"Ready?" she asked.

Not just yet. He turned her face toward his for a welcome-home kiss.

She melted into him for an all-too-brief moment before pulling away with a small, embarrassed smile. "Mark! This is a no-parking zone!"

What is it that's missing? he asked himself as she navigated with great concentration from Southwest Florida International Airport. He honestly didn't know. Watching her drive, with the wind kicking up the sprightly sections of thick brown hair, both arms tanned again and her hands strong on the wheel and gear shift, a smile lingering like a delightful memory on her lips, Mark had no idea what he thought was missing. He tried to dismiss it; had to be the paranoia. Just because he had struck out twice before . . . *Enough, guy. Let it go.*

Tonight, he ascertained that Shelley had gone all out. "You look amazing," he called to her over the rushing wind as they sped a little along the straightaway that led out of the airport. The halter dress, tied with a bow just under her hair, was one of his personal favorites. Dragging his eyes away from contemplating the bare skin at her shoulder, he watched the road, thankful to be home.

"I missed you," she murmured against his shoulder when they'd arrived at his condo. "Glad you're back."

He moved his hands over her skin, enjoying just being with her again. "Me, too."

She leaned back a little, seemed to be about to say something, but then didn't.

He couldn't handle that from her. "Come on," he said, caressing her jaw with one hand. "Out with it."

"Um, I got an e-mail from your sister, Joanna."

Surprised, he laughed out loud. "Really? Was she hounding you about your brother, Shell? You can ignore that stuff, you know. She's a big Diamondbacks fan, but—"

She was shaking her head. "No, not that at all. She was just concerned for *you*."

He closed his eyes. He could guess. "Hurricane season."

"Well, have you got *anything* else to get ready?"

He ran his hands up and down her bare arms, admiring her persistence while feeling annoyed at having an otherwise enjoyable welcome home intruded upon by his kid sister. "Shelley, I just got home. I'm tired. It's been a long day."

"It's eleven o'clock and we both have to work tomorrow, right? I'm fully fit to heft bookcases now, you know," she told him with a grin that held shared memories.

Thankful for her willingness to let it go, he drew her to him. "I'm glad. No one else levels bookcases like you do."

Thirteen

"I know that your dad will do the best he can..."

Shelley was by Dinah's desk, flipping through her calls for the day. It was already hot. Half past seven in the morning and half past eighty degrees and climbing. She had a light day today. Only half a dozen calls. *Thank you, Lord, for air conditioning.*

"Shelley!"

"Dinah, look at you. You're . . . going to pop!"

Now heavily pregnant, the young woman walked slowly to her chair. "I dropped this morning. I can breathe, but I feel like I've got a bowling ball trying to get out."

"Dropped?"

"Oh. The baby dropped. You know, his head settled into the birth canal." Dinah leaned back a little and stretched her legs out in front of her. "He'll show up any day now, is what I'm thinking. I guess I'll be needing those diapers you got me for my shower, huh?"

Shelley had to smile. "Let's hope the *baby* needs them instead, hmm?"

Dinah rolled her eyes. "So . . . How's it going with you and that TDH?"

"Mark? We're still going out, if that's what you want to know." She winked. "And he's still very Tall, very Dark, and very Handsome." Checking her watch, she told Dinah to have a careful day. "And if you do pop while I'm gone, call me."

At her first call—this being Wednesday, she was in North Fort Myers—the customer had the Weather Channel on an enormous flat-screen television. "Did you see that?" the lady wondered. "First named storm of the season."

"Already?" Shelley knelt at the skirt of the sofa to repair the stitching on it. It was particular work, but not mind-consuming. "What's the name?"

"Armando."

"Tropical Storm Armando, huh?" She looked up to see the screen over the arm of the sofa. "Ah, out there in the Atlantic? Let's hope it stays there." Especially with Mark being so stubborn about his storm preparation. *Men!* No, she wasn't going to say a word about Tropical Storm Armando to him. She wanted to see if he would say something first.

She called him when she was on her lunch. Generally, if he was busy, he'd call her back. If not, it was a very pleasant half-hour of conversation if she were on the far side of town. Sometimes, she could cruise by and they had lunch together at his office, or he'd meet her by the river. Today, though, it was a phone call.

"What are we studying tonight?" she asked him, watching the people going in and out of the Target where she had found a nice tree to hide under in the van.

"Actually, our youth is doing something this evening. Should be interesting. Still want to come?" His voice carried his smile to her. "It'd be something, you know, to sit next to the most talented woman I know for an entire hour and a half."

She blushed, glad he didn't see her. "D'you think we could actually hold hands or something?" she teased.

His laugh was like a caress. "Well, maybe. If we're very careful."

"All right. I'll come."

"Call me when you're ready and I'll come for you."

"Wow, curbside service?"

"I'm not teaching. I'll have a few minutes."

After all her calls were done—early, but sometimes it happened that way in the summer—she returned to the warehouse. Dinah was still in the office.

"You're back early."

"Had to make sure you were still pregnant," Shelley retorted. She didn't like losing the hours, but it was part of the job in the summer. Wiping some lingering perspiration from her temples, she set her paperwork on Dinah's desk. "So, anything weird happening tomorrow?"

She got as much advance information as she could before clocking out for the night. Then she hurried home, swallowed something for dinner, and took a shower to get ready for church. If she had been going to her home church for midweek Bible Study, she wouldn't have bothered. They all knew her and Dad well enough to know that they worked, and worked hard, during the week so if they managed to get to church at all, that was the main thing. But going to Mark's church, she felt as if she had to be The Associate Pastor's Girlfriend, too. That meant a shower and something nice to wear, and she liked to check her pedicure to make sure that the meerkats —Mark had let that slip one night and she thought it incredibly funny—had nothing to look at that was objectionable.

"Shelley." He had actually winced when she repeated that term of his. "I'm sorry. I never should have said it."

"But, Mark. It's so descriptive."

Laughing, he acknowledged it was, but he asked her to please try not to use it. "I'd hate to hurt anyone's feelings," he told her.

There was a lot he had to keep in mind, beyond the basic ministry of organizing the different educational programs at his church. Shelley wanted to make sure that she did not do anything that would reflect badly on him.

Eventually, she was sure, it would become easier. It was like learning a new job, she guessed. Skills and preparation would yield results.

She was just applying mascara when her phone rang, with the distinctive "Take Me Out to the Ballgame" tune she saved for Stevie. "Hey, bro!"

"Hey. Just wanted to remind you about the game on Saturday. Is your boyfriend going to make it?"

"Shoot. Can you believe I forgot to ask him?"

"Shell! Yes, I can totally believe that. Ask him. I promise," he said, his deep voice sincere in his own obnoxious, fraternal style, "not to embarrass you guys in front of anyone."

"Gee, thanks. Yeah, I'll ask him. Might be iffy, but I'll try. Sorry I forgot before."

" 'Kay. See you Saturday."

She had only barely applied the mascara when Mark arrived. She jogged down the hall to the front door. "Hi!"

His arms came out automatically, she was sure, to catch her if she stumbled. Her feigned glare to him got an angled look back. "Hi! Running late?"

"Nope. Just had a phone call. You busy Saturday?"

"As in *this* Saturday?"

"Yep. Diamondbacks are playing the Marlins in Miami. Afternoon game. We could get there and back by midnight. I have tickets. Stevie called to remind me. He wants to meet you."

Laughing, he nodded. "All right. You can give me the details on the way to church. Do you have everything?"

"I sure do. Let's go."

One thing she absolutely adored about Mark Countryman was his *manner*. He was a gentleman. *Mom would have adored him, too.*

She watched him get in the car behind the wheel and smile at her. "You look wonderful," he told her. "I like you in red."

It was the first time he had ever stated a preference, so she took immediate mental note. Red knit shirt—with sleeves—that had a tiny satin bow accent at the neckline, and the long white linen skirt. She gave him an obvious once-over. "Thank you. You're not so bad yourself." He'd been at church all day, which meant office wear instead of his more casual attire, but at least he wasn't having to wear a tie. She always felt sorry for a man with a tie in the summer.

At church, she was thankful for his hand around hers as they entered. It was silly, but she liked the reinforcement. Could she ever get used to this?

Oh, probably, but it's going to take a while.

Within moments of entering the building, they were surrounded by inquisitive, friendly women. This was the new pattern of her Wednesday nights.

A classically manicured hand brushed her arm. "Shelley, dear, so good to see you. I was telling Lily, here, about your crocheting."

"Mrs. Southard, good evening," Shelley responded, nodding at Lily Mitchell as well. "You're so kind to remember I do that. What's the occasion?"

Mark spoke softly near her ear. "Shell? I'm going to check with Tyler and make sure everything's up for tonight." Tyler was the youth pastor.

"Okay." She returned to politely conversing with the ladies, though she couldn't help following Mark with her eyes.

Jacob Cairns and his wife came by next, and Annie Keller, and Kristi and her husband. All of them, it seemed, were determined to make her feel as normal and welcome as possible. Even the problematic Customer Cairns—not a customer at present—was far less formidable with his wife at his elbow and without Important Businessman shouting from his demeanor. He was different here in the congregation.

"Did you see the Weather Channel?" Kristi's husband asked her as his wife joined Mark, Ben, and Tyler off elsewhere. Probably to pray, Shelley guessed, before the youth presentation this evening. "They got a name to that storm now."

"Armando, I heard. Another one's kicking up, too."

"Weird, isn't it?" he asked with a crooked smile, running a hand over his shock of almost orange hair. He was a thin, pale man, originally from Iowa, and he helped lead worship on Sunday mornings. She had only seen him do so on Easter.

"Why weird?"

"Well, it seems like all of us—like you and me and half of everyone I meet, practically—that move here from somewhere else become amateur meteorologists, you know?"

She nodded, completely understanding. "Wish my Mark would, too," she murmured.

"Well, so far, so good, right?"

"Did you see the water temperatures in the Gulf, though? They're warm this year."

"Yeah. Well. Let's pray for another quiet season."

"Definitely."

Mark and Kristi rejoined them, and Shelley put her storm-ward thoughts away. Mark had one huge stubborn streak and she wasn't going to push him on it here at church on a Wednesday night.

He made a point of taking her hand, his fingers wrapping around hers with warm intent. "Everything all right?"

"Just fine," she told him. "Even better now that you're back. You?"

His back to everyone that was finding their seats in the pews, he lifted her hand to his lips and kissed it. "Even better, now that I'm with you," he whispered above her skin. His breath made her shiver and she smiled, looking down.

If there were some happily interested pairs of eyes that followed them as they found a seat near the front of the worship center, Shelley was getting used to it. She concentrated on enjoying the rare sense of rightness that came when she got to worship at Mark's side instead of apart from him, separated either by their different churches or his own job requirements.

After all, she loved the man. From his stubborn streak to that deadly dimple and everything in between. *Thank you, Lord God. Thank you so much.* The sudden welling of feeling had her blinking as the lights changed to accent the young people on the front platform.

"Are you all right?" Mark whispered near her ear.

She nodded, not trusting herself to speak. She could only lift his hand and press it to her cheek. *I love you,* she mouthed in the near darkness. *I just wish I was brave enough to tell you.*

"Oh please, Mark. If you can, okay? I mean, you know, no pressure, but please?"

"Joanna. Come on, this is Shelley's brother."

"And you're her *boyfriend*. Significant Other. Whatever it is you feel like calling yourself, you're it. Can't you at least maybe ask *her* to ask him?"

"No. If I feel I can ask for his autograph, I will. I'm not going to ask her to do it for me."

She took it with decent grace, he guessed as they eventually said goodbye. Just in time, too. He shut off the earpiece for his phone and tucked it in the center console of his car as he pulled up to Shelley's house. He was looking forward to going to the baseball game. It seemed kind of strange that he had never been to one before.

He just could not believe that Joanna was being so pushy about the autograph thing. He hoped that she wasn't annoying Shelley with her opportunism.

"Mark!" Shelley greeted him at the door, wearing a red Diamondbacks team jersey with her brother's name on the back. Not just a souvenir either, he was guessing. Might have even been Steve Roberts's game jersey, in a prior season. She also had a baseball cap and even a glove. "Good morning."

He took off her cap so he could kiss her smiling lips properly. "Good morning to you, too. I should have known you'd have all the paraphernalia." Smiling, he gestured to the glove she carried. "What's with the ribbon, though?"

"Oh, you know, just in case I do something stupid and throw it or lose it. I'll know it's mine."

Chuckling, he kept those increasingly heavy three words on his tongue, but pulled her close anyway. "You're incredible," he said instead, breathing in her warmth and the unique blend of scents that meant *Shelley* to his senses. There was something indescribably precious about having her this close to him.

It had been decided that they would all travel in the Roberts's Lincoln on the way out to Miami's Dolphin Stadium, where the Florida Marlins had their home games. The Diamondbacks would be visiting, which meant that they were not getting box seats, but Shelley's brother had managed to cadge some Infield MVP seats, which was pretty good. "We'll be behind home plate, but up a few rows. It's a great view," she had said.

Conversation on the two-plus hour trip sped and slowed. Sometimes it seemed as if Shelley and her father had months of catching up to do. Sometimes it was shop-talk. Other times, he could see how Shelley worked to include Stephanie in the conversations. He was reminded that the older woman had joined the family comparatively recently. Shelley and her dad had been on their own for many years.

"Shell," Stephanie said after a lull of several miles. "Did you catch the Weather Channel before you came?"

Mark felt like sighing heavily. Had Shelley put them up to this? No, she seemed uncomfortable, too, as she answered. "No, what's up?"

"That other tropical disturbance that formed yesterday? They're calling her Bianca now."

"Well," Shelley said, sounding conciliatory, "at least Armando is out spinning in the Atlantic all by himself."

Mark pushed out a breath. "That's a relief."

Shelley squeezed his hand and offered him a small smile before addressing Stephanie again. "Did you guys decide what you're going to do on your vacation?"

Stephanie turned a little under her seatbelt, her clear blue eyes alight with anticipation. "Yes. Sorry, we meant to tell you, but . . ."

Mark nodded. "I know. I've been keeping her a little busy lately."

"Not complaining," Stephanie assured him with a little laugh. "But we're going up to South Carolina, Shell. Looking for some property. Maybe for a vacation home for now, and for retirement later."

"Retirement . . ." Shelley seemed a bit stunned. "Wow. Hadn't really thought about that for y'all, you know?" she said, an accent sliding into her voice that Mark remembered was very rare for her. "Well, take pics, okay? So I know where to find you."

They reached the field in plenty of time to angle for parking and find their seats before the start of the game. When the players came out for the National Anthem, Shelley discreetly pointed Steve out on the baseline. The blond second baseman must have known where they were, for he looked over their seating area and nodded at them.

"So, what's the plan again?" Mark asked during a mid-inning transition later in the game. The Diamondbacks had just scored two runs, with her brother on deck. He guessed Stevie Roberts would be up first in the next inning.

Shelley turned to him, a bag of overpriced peanuts in her hand. They probably cost a full dollar more in the seats than inside, but she had insisted that was part of the fun of it all. "The plan? Oh, after the game? What's the matter, Mark? Bored already?" She was teasing, but he saw the concern in the clear brown gaze and shook his head.

"Not at all. I just wondered. You're not the only one who likes prep time, right?"

She dropped her head, color washing over her face. "Um, sorry."

Catching her chin on his fingers, he lifted her face. "Don't be. You're priceless."

Her lips parted, but she pulled away, obviously flustered. "Um. The plan. Right. Well. After the game, Steve will call and let us know where he's got reservations." She smiled a little and looked to the field, where her brother was stationing himself near second base. "We'll meet him there. After dinner, I guess we'll pile back in the car and head home." Then, with a mischievous light in her eye, she asked, "Did Joanna ask you for something, maybe?"

He rolled his eyes. "You two must be exchanging e-mails every day."

"Almost!"

In spite of his annoyance, he had to chuckle. "Sounds just like her. And you. If she gets to be a bother—"

"Mark," she said, placing her hand on his cheek. "She's your sister. I think she's great."

He caught her hand under his palm and kept it there for a moment, just enjoying the feeling of being a *couple*, away from everything that usually surrounded them. It was relaxing.

Later, the compulsory tourist activity was the seventh inning trip for something to drink. Steve hadn't hit one out of the park that evening, but the Diamondbacks were comfortably over the Marlins by five runs, so Shelley dragged Mark out of their seats. "C'mon . . . You have to. It's practically mandatory."

"How did I survive all these years without completing all these mandatory activities?" he inquired of the air behind her head as she led him up the stairs to one of the wonderfully air-conditioned venues with food and drinks and assorted Marlin merchandise for sale.

She stopped and leaned against a wall, smiling up at him. "How did you survive? I have no idea. But I'm really glad you did."

Hand in hand, they strolled the concourse and he again had the sense of relishing this as a special time. A rarity, since nowhere would there be anyone who would pull him aside or call his name. He enjoyed what he did, he was called to the ministry and he felt secure in that calling, but sometimes it was nice to have a break. He wondered if Shelley felt the same, but he didn't want to ruin the pleasant time with a potentially awkward conversation.

She didn't buy anything. She was here, he could tell, purely for the experience. Television screens displayed the game for those who were here, but while the announcement was made for re-commencement of the game, it was interrupted on alternate screens.

"Great," he groused. "Another tropical update."

"Mark . . ." Shelley's voice was careful, but he felt a frustration boiling out of proportion to the circumstances. He could only look at her and hope she could see it in his eyes. Hers narrowed. "Fine. Be that way," she said on a sigh. "I won't even look at it."

She deliberately turned around and walked away, avoiding looking at *any* of the screens, even though her brother was again on deck to bat and could be seen on the stadium monitors.

He hurried to reach her. "Hey," he said, catching her hand and tugging gently so she'd stop her almost headlong rush to get back to their seats. "I'm sorry, Shell. I really don't mean to make you so frustrated."

Frustrated. *He* was the one who was frustrated. What was it? He took both her hands in his and kissed her lightly on the forehead. "Forgive me?"

"Of course. You don't even have to ask, Mark."

"I do," he assured her, very seriously.

"I—I'll try to stop nagging. I really will."

"And I'll try to stop getting irritated if I think you are, all right?"

She laughed a little and leaned into him. Wrapping his arms around her, he restrained a sigh of his own and hoped that their combined worries and frustrations would be left behind them for the time being.

Relieved, Mark felt able to enjoy dinner with her brother at a high-walled booth in a fashionable corner of Miami after the game was over. He was a boisterous young man, older than Shelley by a few years, who came prepared with a game ball already signed: *For Joanna from Steve Roberts.*

When they left the restaurant, Mark shook Steve Jr.'s hand again. "Thank you for the ball for my sister. She'll probably leave me her children in her will or something."

The heavily-muscled ballplayer threw back his head and laughed. "Oh, no. Maybe I should take it back?"

Shelley hugged her brother and said they'd wait for Steve Sr. and Stephanie at the car. "I just needed some space to breathe," she confessed to Mark quietly as they reached the gleaming Lincoln.

He held her next to his chest, feeling an overwhelming wish to be close to her. "Me, too," he murmured into her hair. "Me, too."

How many ways did he love this woman? *Lord? I wish—I know I said I don't want what you don't want for me, but Lord! I want her. Have I chosen the wrong girl again?*

Fourteen

"Pray for him to choose well."

Sunday proceeded according to the usual routines, and Shelley tried to take comfort in that. Tried not to heed the anxious place in her middle as she checked over her hurricane shutters. She had gone with clear Lexan panels for the larger windows in the living room, and regular aluminum panels for the other windows of her home. They were each cut to fit the different windows, and she had the metal shutters marked with a permanent marker so she would know which went where. All she would have to do, should this turn out to be a busy hurricane season after all, would be to install all the braces for each set of shutters in advance. Mounting them in the advent of an immediate threat would be much simpler.

Tropical Storm Bianca was on track to make her presence known on Cuba within twenty-four hours. If she went into the warm waters of the Gulf of Mexico after that, it was possible for her to take a track similar to Cyrus's, the meteorologists said. Some of that was hype, but Shelley listened anyway.

When Mark came to pick her up for church that evening, she tried one more time to talk to him. His "hello" embrace seemed a bit distracted. Not absent-minded exactly, but rather as if he were thinking about something else in conjunction with her. She didn't understand it, but had learned months ago that asking him a deep and meaningful, non-theological question on a Sunday was a bad idea. He had Bible studies on the brain, Scripture verses connecting with other ones in his head like a huge puzzle, and other things he probably couldn't even talk to her about, due to ministerial confidentiality. He had that kind of job.

Still, she tried to make conversation as he settled her in his car. "So, do we have plans for tomorrow?" They had reached this place in their relationship and she liked it. A place where he didn't have to plan elaborate outings to impress her. He had to know she was way past "impressed" and on her way to "committed".

She was there already, but they had not yet reached *that* point in their relationship, she supposed, to discuss it. Waiting and preparing had served her well and, as long as he was happy, she was happy. Except, he didn't seem entirely happy this afternoon.

His smile was generic, but again, it was Sunday. "Plans? Nothing I can think of offhand. There's that movie sequel you wanted to see. We can catch a *matinée* if you want." He caught her eye. "Every girl under thirty is practically drooling over that guy."

She scoffed. "Every girl under thirty drools on her pillow, too, at some point or other. He's totally not my type," she told him with a saucy toss of her head. "I prefer my men older and wiser, as you should know." Then she mentally chewed herself out. This was not where she wanted to take the discussion today. "Um, no. So, how about you come help me put up my storm braces on the windows instead? I have to put them up tomorrow, and I could use another pair of hands, if yours are available. Are they?" she asked with a suggestive lilt to her voice.

The sigh of the long-suffering pervaded his entire car. "All right. To spend the day with you, I'll try my hand at helping you with your all-important storm preparations." A slanted smile and shake of his handsome head. "On one condition," he added with a look.

"What?"

"Please, no Weather Channel tomorrow, all right?"

It wasn't exactly what she had been hoping for, but—"All right."

"*Thank* you."

At his church, she was able to greet more people by name now. She was happy to ask after children and job situations, and complimented women on shoes and purses and colors. She was also able to "talk shop" with a couple of the men, who still seemed surprised that she, a woman with snazzy shoes and a bow-decorated headband, could chime in intelligently on a discussion of DeWalt versus Makita power tools.

The following morning, Mark was slated to come over early so they could complete the outside work before the day got insanely hot. It was mid-July and only someone with a desire to experience heatstroke up close and personal wanted to work outside in the afternoon. The plan was to go swimming at his place afterward. Being only human, Shelley was unsurprised to realize that she was nervous about this. The pool was public —she had seen it—surrounded by a low, white, wrought-iron fence so that the view of the Caloosahatchee was unimpeded. It was not a large pool by any means. Just big enough to cool off in on a summer afternoon. Her nerves stemmed from the idea of anyone—especially Dr. Mark Countryman —seeing her in a swimsuit in such a non-swimsuit environment. She usually reserved the swimsuit for the beach, where she and other people, who held no romantic or sexual attraction for her in any way, could sunbathe and play volleyball or swim. On the beach, a swimsuit was standard attire. Unless you were really *hot* or really *not*, no one paid you any heed. Shelley knew she was neither hot nor not on the beaches of South Florida.

But in a pool with Mark? *The water had better be really cool in that pool . . .*

Time for the latest on Tropical Storm Bianca, she decided before Mark arrived. A quick check and a few minutes told her that while Armando had spun himself into a mere Tropical Depression harmlessly east of the Bahamas, Bianca had actually strengthened a little and was beginning to be known in Cuba.

She could, in fact, be a hurricane within a day.

"And look at that track," she said. "Should call Dad . . . No, wait, he and Steph are off to South Carolina for a week. Right. Well, I'll call later. Let 'em have their day. Should check his house, though. Maybe Mark might want to come?"

His knock came while she was still engrossed in the path of Tropical Storm Bianca. She leapt up to answer the door, still seeing the possible paths of the storm in front of her eyes. "Hi, Mark."

"Are you all right?" He glanced at her television and she winced.

"Sorry." She clicked her remote to turn off the television. "Sorry, I promised. I was just distracted."

He put his arms around her and she held him close. "Shelley," he murmured. "I'm sorry. You shouldn't have to be so worried about—about all of that. Or about me. Really." He smiled a little, yesterday's preoccupation nowhere in evidence. "If I gave you any other impression, I apologize. I've been—" He stopped, seeming to search for the right word.

"Stressed? I've noticed," she told him, leaning back to watch his face, study the small lines around his eyes, the texture of his skin. He met her scrutiny with some of his own. "In spite of, you know, all the recent improvements," she went on, planting a couple of chaste kisses along his jaw, "I do hope we're still friends. I mean, I hope you can talk to me if something's bothering you. I know I'm maybe not exactly the perfect confidante, but I—I do care about you." *More than I can tell you.*

A certain gravity swept his features. A thoughtfulness that made her feel that whatever it was, as she had thought before, had to do with her. Maybe he was still hung up on the age thing? Could be. She didn't know. Perhaps it would be a good day to talk about it?

He put the kibosh on that one with a sudden flash of a smile. "All right. I promised to be another set of hands for you, right? Put me to work."

Later then. When it was hot and they weren't working. Later would serve just as well to discuss the age difference. "All right, then. C'mon. It's not a touristy thing, but this whole storm-shutter business is also part of the Florida Experience," she told him, with Over-the-Top Tour Guide in every nuance of her voice.

They distributed the mounting brackets at the different windows first, and then she bolted them in, with his help to keep everything stable.

"You did *not* need my assistance," he stated unequivocally while they took a water break some time later. Wiping his forehead, he smiled at her. "Sometimes, I look at you with your work-gear or hear you talking about tools at church and have to laugh, you know."

"Why?" She was not affronted, just amused that he was amused.

"I guess I will always have two really vivid images of you, side by side in my head. One, honestly, is of you in that dress you were wearing at Costco. You said you were a very—what was that term?—girly girl. Right. And the other is of you lifting that bookcase in my office the first day you were there, remember?" The light in his dark gaze was as hot as the day, and she felt shy and rather proud that she could provoke such warmth in him.

"Oh, you bet. I had found out Mr. TDH had a name! I'll never forget that day."

He burst out in a surprised laugh. "What?"

Color flooding her face, she couldn't keep her own grin hidden. "TDH. Tall, Dark, and Handsome. Um, that's what I called you at work, you know, when I was talking to one of the girls in Customer Service." She eyed him closely. "Are you blushing, Dr. Countryman?"

"I think I am," he said slowly. "I, ah, thank you. Never considered myself in that category before."

"Well, I have from the moment I first saw you."

He brushed her cheek with the back of his hand. "Thank you."

"I'm thinking I want to run to my dad's house," Shelley told Mark after they had finished with her windows.

"Aren't they in South Carolina?" he asked, wanting her to know that he had been paying attention.

At her dining table, they were just starting on a quick lunch of sandwiches and a soda, while the sun poured in through the sliding arcadia glass doors. The promise of a dip in the pool was looking better every moment, he mused with a private smile as he traced the line of Shelley's shoulder with his eyes. He had never considered himself a "shoulder man" before meeting her, but the strong, feminine lines seemed to draw his gaze whenever they were together.

"They are, yeah, but I don't know if he got his shutters out and ready. That storm is—" Stopping herself with fingers over her lips, she met his eyes. He was irritated at the guilt he read there. Irritated with *himself,* because he had been so frustrated before as to make her think she had to refrain from discussing the storms in front of him.

"Sweetheart," he began, taking her hand. "Please don't look like that. I'm not going to bite your head off because you're worried. But you shouldn't *be* worried, you know? What are the odds?"

"Odds don't mean a thing in storm-tracking, Mark," she said, sliding her hand from his and getting to her feet. "You should see the pictures I have from when the *odds* sent Cyrus farther north."

He got to his feet, too, following her down the hall. "Shelley."

"No, this is serious, Mark," she called over her shoulder. "Let me just get you a CD with some of the pics, okay? Look at them when you feel like it, but I'd like to go check my dad's house before we do anything else."

He stopped at the door of a small room and leaned against the frame. He hadn't seen this room before. A computer occupied one corner, and a beanbag chair puddled invitingly near another, where a storage cube set of various colors of yarn sat with an air of neglect. Shelley was a woman of many talents, he knew, but he didn't think it was a good time of year for crocheting.

"I might even need to put the shutters up," she was saying, flipping through a stack of CD cases next to her computer. "Just in case Bianca comes this way." Yellow jewel case in hand, she eyed him from across the room. "And Mark, I really, really think you should let me at least look at your windows and all that. Your place is right in a Category One flood zone."

Suddenly, he had *had* it with the storm talk. Already frustrated by his lingering confusion about what the Lord's intentions were with Shelley in his life, Mark was also irritated at her persistence in worrying and at the echoes of his family's expressed concern. The combination pulsed at him fiercely all at once.

"Stop it," he ground out. "Just stop it. I'm forty years old, Shelley. I've managed to make it this far without becoming absolutely paranoid about storm tracking. I really have. I was an adult and taking care of myself when you were still in elementary school. I do *not* need to hear what I have to do to make it through my third hurricane season here in Florida. Not from you, not from anyone. If I get flooded out, I guess I'll just have to manage, like everyone else will, right?"

He saw her face blanch, her features scrunch together, and heard the catch in her breath. "M-Mark? I'm only saying—"

"You're only saying what you've been saying since we *met*, Shelley. Thing is, I'm not going to worry about it. I'm going to just live my life without that kind of—of fear hanging over it." Couldn't she see that the worry was a bad idea for her? For anyone? "No one should have to live like that."

She lost her pallor and went all red. "Go. Just go, okay?" She pointed in patent dismissal. "I—I'm only trying to help, Mark. Just wanting you to be safe. To keep your stuff safe, too."

"Shelley, it's just stuff," he said, trying to step toward her, ignoring her ire to try to reason with her now that his flash of angry frustration had vented.

"Lives are more important."

"Sure. But so are the memories! You have no idea, Mark. None. None *whatsoever*. Just go." Tears tracked down her cheeks and she held up one hand as he tried, again, to cross the room to her. "No. You've made yourself very clear. Just go. I can check on my dad's house without you. As you pointed out," she added, her voice dripping with derision, "I do *not* need your help." She wiped her face dry and stared at him, her eyes strangely flat and empty.

"Shelley."

"Go! Now! Or do you need me to remind you where the door is?"

He studied her face, remorse flooding his whole body. "All right." He needed to compose himself. To think of what to say to her. "I'm going. Just . . . Just take care, okay?" There they were, those three heavy words, but they were sealed behind a cold wall of guilt for having made her so upset.

So, after a moment, he turned to go. He would try calling later when they had both cooled off.

He was outside and getting into his car when her door opened again with a reckless sound. "Mark?"

Hope flared in his heart for just a moment and he stepped toward her. Maybe he wouldn't have to wait to apologize. Maybe, like his, her temper had flared and blew out and—

"Take this CD anyway. Take it," she insisted, stalking to his side, the case thrust before her like a dead thing she wanted to dispose of. "If you think it's *worth* anything, just look at what *isn't* so important," she said. "See what can happen when the odds you were talking about come out and you lose."

He took the CD, saw the words *Life After Cyrus* on it, and nodded. "All right."

"Fine. And then you can send it to Joanna. She wanted to see some pics." Shelley's consideration for his sister, even now, made him want to reach for her again. Her flat expression, though, put that idea down. "At least *she* has some sense about these things. You . . . you take care, too," she added much more softly.

Waiting until she was back indoors again, Mark sat behind the wheel of his car. Kicking himself. The sunlight had caught on a fresh rim of tears in her eyes before she turned away.

He knew how that felt, because his own eyes burned, too.

Fifteen

"We promised we would."

She collapsed just inside her front door, waiting to hear his car go away. Waiting to be alone. Waiting.

"Oh, God . . ." she whimpered, feeling the pressure that had just exploded within try to explode out of her, too. "Oh, God . . ." She leaned her head back until it hit the door. Crying as she hadn't let herself do in ages. Maybe even since her mother died. "Oh, God . . . Help me . . . Help him. Help us, *please.*"

Never did it occur to her that this was the last she would see him. Not once. But to hear his rejection of all that she was trying to do to keep him safe, that *hurt*. A lot. Sliced right through her. Would have drawn blood if the mind and body were as closely attuned as some cable television gurus thought they were.

And the age reference again. She groaned and hit her knee with one hand. "Knew I should've talked to him before!" She gasped with the self-realization. "Knew it." But would it have changed his opinion? He was older and wiser, and she did appreciate that, but he did not make it a practice to point it out to her. Ever. Until just now.

That hurt, too. *Slice.*

Then, a memory slipped through her helplessness and tears, and she felt a smile. "At least I'm not asking the *why* question," she murmured out loud with a sniffle. That made her remember their first kiss. Though there had been countless others since, that one had been the first and she would always remember it.

Closing her eyes, she allowed herself to become boneless for a few moments. Calming herself. Breathing. She didn't even know if he loved her, but still . . . This was a relationship that could go somewhere. It was. And she was remembering what her mother had told her.

She rolled up to her feet and jogged to her room. The letter. She'd find her mother's last letter to her just for the encouragement. *Then* she would go to her dad's house.

"Thank you, Lord," she remembered to say, hiccoughing and red-eyed though she was. "Thank you. For hope. It's not fear. It's not uncaring. It's just that he doesn't get it. I know that. How patient you are with us. How forgiving. I have to be, too."

Still . . . She glanced upward and told the Lord her God, "I'm *not* calling him."

She did, though, call her father. "Dad?"

He chuckled. "Shell. Never expected to hear from you today, it bein' Monday and all."

She bit her lip and hunched into a smaller package in the middle of her bed. It was a queen-sized bed covered with bedding in a bright ribbon and flower motif she had seen on sale as a Last Season purchase. Expensive store, serious mark-down. She loved it. "Yeah, well. You know. Mark was over earlier actually. Helping me with my mounting brackets."

"How'd he do?" Dad knew that Mark had only a passing acquaintance with power tools.

In spite of the pain that still lashed in faint echoes within her, she had to smile ruefully. "He did pretty good, Dad. But that's not why I'm calling. I didn't know if you'd been watching the storm cone projections."

"Not today," he allowed, his voice giving her a hint that maybe, perhaps, she had interrupted something. She blushed and would have apologized, but he continued. "But I know how it is, Shell. So if you feel you need to batten down our hatches too, you know where everything is."

In a hurry now to let him return to his vacation and his wife, Shelley forced herself to sound as pleasant and upbeat as possible. "Will do. Thanks, Dad. Um, sorry to have intruded on your vacation."

His laugh was sincere, with no awkward overtones that she could hear. "Have a good week, Shell. We'll keep our eyes on the Gulf, don't worry."

Ending the connection, Shelley sat in the soundlessness of the heated afternoon as it streamed through her window curtains, not heeding time as it passed. Just trying to make sure that she had done her best earlier. She certainly had not been prepared for the anger she had heard in Mark's voice. The frustration. As if he had reached his absolute limit of endurance with her in this regard.

She sighed. *I promised to try not to be a nag about it.*

And she had broken that promise. Mark did, she admitted to herself, have a point. A very tiny one, but a point.

But so did she.

In the absolute stillness of the moment, she sighed again, feeling the loneliness settle like a physical presence around her.

When she had been a young girl, her mother had gone from her. When she was a teenager, her brother had crossed the country, never to be a part of her daily life again. It had been just her and her father for years thereafter. And then, he had taken a wife and she, Shelley, had moved to a place of her own. Though a part of their lives, as they were a part of hers, when one came down to it, she lived a very solitary life.

The loneliness weighed heavily on her now. The memory of Mark's face, his harsh tone, his tossing her youth up at her . . . "Oh, God," she said again, her voice shaky with uncertainty. "What do I do now?"

Do not let the sun go down on your anger. The remembered verse came immediately to mind. She examined it a little. Decided she had several hours leeway, and she was not going to tell him she was sorry for kicking him out of her house when he had insulted her. At least, not yet.

Lips set in a firm line, she rose from her bed and went to her mirror. The red rims of her eyes wouldn't be seen by anyone that mattered anyway, right? No. "What am I gonna do?" she asked her frazzled reflection. "What else? I'm going to get ready for Bianca."

He didn't go home. Not right away. Instead, he went to the river. It being a Monday afternoon in the middle of summer, there were few folks down there. It wasn't a big time for fishing and people were working, so there were only a couple of presumed retirees parking and walking to the restaurant attached to the hotel.

Shelley had told him that that happened. They had seen it. Together. Right here. This would often happen during one of her oddly-timed, dovetailed lunch breaks. She had an irregular work schedule for someone who liked to be prepared for the future.

He appreciated her commitment to preparation, but he believed sincerely that a person had to have faith, too. Faith that the Lord God would hold them up in the face of adversity. Faith that, even in a disaster, they weren't alone. Faith was the bedrock of his life—he thought it was hers, too, but she was so insistent upon inserting *herself* into the equation instead of relying fully on God.

Impulsively, Mark sat down and took off his socks and shoes—he had been wearing serious footgear to work outside with Shelley and her windows. Tucking the socks into the toes of his low hiking boots, he carried them as he walked to the lapping waves of the Caloosahatchee. The river did seem to have more life to it today. Maybe, though, he was imagining it.

Birds were seeking shelter in the shade offered by the trees, down the beach. Here, he was mostly alone as he stepped carefully with his bare feet in the cool water.

He didn't know what to think. He knew what he wanted, he knew what he yearned for and whom, but—*I should have told her how I feel,* he decided with sudden clarity. *I should have.* Was it as much cowardice as caution that had compelled him not to tell her the depth of his feelings for her? Sometimes, he really did wonder how he deserved her. Oh, when he was younger . . . But he hadn't told Dawn either, had he? All those years ago—he had kept his feelings to himself then, too.

Which had, come to think of it, worked out for the very best. She never knew and he was glad of that. Never more so than when she and Garrison had spent that week down here in April.

He should have told Shelley. There was no other man to think of, no children involved. Just a man and a woman. A woman who was above anyone else in his mind and heart. She was utterly unique in all of God's creation.

And he had disparaged her to her face and belittled her concerns for him.

Regret clutched at his insides, bringing with it actual physical pain. *Lord . . . Why didn't you stop me?*

When had he given the Lord the opportunity? When? When had he stopped to pray, to ask for a moment to think? No, he had just let that very human irritation and very masculine aversion to—*Yes, she is, but you know you love her anyway*—a repetitive female hold full sway over his thoughts and words and deeds.

Only for a few moments, but the damage was done. Judging by the look on her face, his words had given more pain than she had felt even when her bones had been broken.

"And James is her favorite book of the Bible," he murmured, struck by the sideways irony. She had discussed and internalized the notion of taming the tongue. She was concerned about any position that placed her as a teacher, due to the admonitions to be found in that same book. She, who appreciated the very unveiled quality to that man's writing, had been hurt, inadvertently, by the man who had taught a seminar on all of the above. *God Almighty, I am so unworthy. Help me. Please.*

Mark had reached the edge of the beach before the rocky little bay that was revealed at lower tide levels. He turned and made his way back, stepping more quickly. *Lord, forgive me for not, not taking you with me on that one. For not taking that moment I should have to ask for guidance before I blew it. Forgive me for hurting this daughter of yours.*

New pain washed over him and he didn't really understand the tears that leapt to his eyes. Was it the reminder that she was a daughter of God, but had no mother to turn to when the man in her life had acted like an insensitive jerk? *Forgive me.*

He was assured of the Lord's forgiveness, but not so sure about Shelley's. Returning to the bench where he had taken off his shoes, he let his feet dry before putting on the boots again. While they dried, he thought, prayed, and thought some more as the sun dipped toward the west and his stomach reminded him that he had, surprisingly, managed to stay out for some hours.

Lord, I want only what you want for me. I do. And if Shelley is not the one, I'll listen. You've brought me through heartbreak before. But Father God in Heaven . . . I would ask that she would be. He remembered his idea of gift wrap and sighed. It seemed foolish now. Now, when he wasn't even positive how she felt. Or how she had felt before this afternoon. *Still, Lord, she's right. I'm not asking* why, *only* how.

He was over-thinking this, he knew. *Stop it. Either you're going to risk it or you're not.*

Risk what? He just wished he knew for sure.

Do not put the Lord your God to the test, he heard in his mind.

What test? he asked silently.

In his mind, he heard his remembered prayer about ribbons and bows and felt a cold mantle of shame drop over his shoulder. "Was *that* what I was doing?" he whispered.

Well, if he wasn't going to do that, what else did he have to go by, save his heart? That was Shelley's already.

Is it really that simple? Mark wondered.

Blowing out a surprised, relieved breath, he felt a certain peace sweep under his skin.

He would go to Shelley. Ask her forgiveness. If she did forgive him, he would finally free those famous three little words he had been keeping to himself. The possibility gladdened his heart.

If she didn't throw him out of her house again, he planned on making a formal proposal as well. He had to be ready for that, too.

"I guess I have some preparations of my own to make," he mused, more at ease now that he had decided to see what had been right in front of him the whole time.

It was nearly sunset by the time Shelley had wrestled her new storm shutters into place on her windows. No one else on the street—none of the occupied homes anyway—had storm shutters up. Yet. But she would be working again tomorrow and could not count on having the time necessary to do the job on her own after work should it become mandatory for her sense of safety.

She had to laugh at her own pride, though, as she used a knee and elbow to do the job another pair of hands could have done if she hadn't kicked them out. Along with the man to whom they belonged. "Yes," she admitted, wiping sweat from her forehead with her forearm. "I could indeed use the help." She didn't *need* it, no, but it would have been *nice*. Otherwise, she did not regret telling Mark to go away. It had, she still felt, been the right response.

Finished at last, she shielded her eyes to watch the sun over the tops of the palm trees. The sun was *setting*. Was she still angry at Mark? Where was he? What was he doing?

"Not watching the Weather Channel," she muttered, shaking off the wistfulness that swept briefly over her. She still had work to do. She was glad to do it, too. Otherwise who knew what she would be up to? Part of her longed to go to him. Knock on the door. Pretend their fight had never happened and ask if the swimming option was still open. Just to see what he would do. The notion appealed to her, but she refrained.

Her dad's place had a pool and she had storm shutters to hang before she collapsed from exhaustion. For she had every intention of exhausting herself. She would work, then swim, then go to bed and wake up, and then go to work tomorrow. Glad that she was scheduled to be in Naples and not North Fort Myers, there would be no opportunity to confront Mark in an inappropriate time or place.

Tucking her swimsuit in a tote bag with some other odds and ends she would want for a post-swimming shower, she resolutely turned off all the lights and went through the kitchen to the garage, where her Mini waited with its top down.

"You," she said to her car with an appreciative pat, "are exactly what I need right now."

It took her until long after dark to finish installing her father's storm shutters. He had some work lights that she utilized as she went around the house. She scrounged in Stephanie's kitchen, though it had been mostly cleaned out before they left for South Carolina. She found a toaster pastry and some orange juice before changing and hitting the pool.

Without the job in front of her, without the need to prepare, to keep busy, to work, Shelley was very much afraid the waves of loneliness that had started after Mark left would get to be too overwhelming for her. She was not going to call him. She was *not*. Period. Even though the sun had gone down. She wasn't really mad, was she?

Before dozing off in the darkness of her father's house, she sighed. "I'm sorry, Lord. I'll do better tomorrow."

Sixteen

"So whenever . . . things get rough around the edges . . . work with it."

"Mark? Dr. Countryman? Are you all right?" Letty's voice reached through the agitated layer that was wrapped around his brain, but only barely.

"Sorry, Letty," he said, stopping at her desk on his way back to his office. He felt like he wasn't even there. The morning shower and shave had happened, but he couldn't even remember going through the motions. "What? Did I miss something?"

Coming around her desk, the faint scent of honeysuckle preceding her, his secretary was frowning. "You look like you missed your bed last night." Then her eyes widened in chagrin. "Not that I am implying anything, Mark! I only mean that your eyes need their own luggage tags, you know?" She placed a hand on his forehead. "No, no fever. But you look terrible." She leaned back. "Were you watching that hurricane all night or something? I used to do that my first hurricane season here."

"When was that?" he wondered absently.

"Two-thousand five. It was a busy year."

"Hmm," he managed, thinking of Shelley. Still. All night. Where was she? "Has Shelley Roberts called this morning?" he asked Letty.

Pursing her lips, she returned to her chair. "Uh, no, Dr. Countryman. Mark. No." She studied him openly. "Is she all right? Are you two all right?" she inquired with some hesitancy.

He didn't answer out loud, but let his face speak for him. "If she calls," he said, sincerely hoping she would, "put her through, all right?"

"Won't she call on your cell?"

Mark rubbed at his tired face. "I haven't a clue, to be honest. All right. I'm here. Do we have any coffee?"

It was good this morning. Strong. He needed that after last night. *Where are you?* he wondered. All night. All morning. He had even called the local emergency rooms. She wasn't at China Town—he had been there too, for dinner and an extra box—not at her house either. He had checked. Knocked on her door, rang the bell. All her windows were shuttered, but the front ones were done in that clear stuff. Nothing. No sign of life in there anywhere. He had wondered, at that point, if she had just collapsed in exhaustion. She hadn't even answered her phone.

He still didn't know where she was, but hoped that she had gone to her father's house. He planned on checking on her there, after her work day would be over, in case she had decamped in an effort to avoid him.

It didn't sound like something she would do, but . . . Powering up his computer, he remembered the CD of pictures Shelley had given him yesterday. He hadn't looked at it yet. He had been too worried to sit and look at pictures, for goodness's sake. She wasn't answering her e-mail, wasn't online, wasn't answering her phone. An idea hit him, and he slipped her card—the one she had given him back in March—from his desk. The receptionist answered and he asked to be transferred to Customer Service.

"Hello, this is Dinah." The voice sounded as if its owner were in the middle of painting a room or something. "Can I help you?"

"Hello, yes, I hope so. Do you know Shelley Roberts?"

"Sir, she's one of our service techs, but is unavailable for our customers to call. If you have a message, I can forward it to her."

"Did she make it in this morning?"

"Yes. Sir? May I ask who's calling?"

Why not? "Of course. This is Mark Countryman." He told her the name of the church and gave her the phone number. "I was just wanting to know if Shelley made it in today, is all."

There was a strange pause on the other side of the line. Then, "Oh, wait! She did some work for that church a few months ago, right?"

"Yes . . ."

Another pause. Then, her voice much more quiet and secretive, she asked, "Are you the *Mark* she's been seeing for a while? The one who wrote the book?"

"That's me. Please, Dinah. I am sorry to bother you, but you said she made it in. Was she all right?"

"Well, yes. She was. I can't really say more than that, but I will say," she went on in that hushed tone, "that she looked really tired."

Relief sank into him from the skin inward, all over. All at once. "Thank you."

Then she made some sort of strange, startled sound. And swore. Loudly. Concerned, Mark asked her what was wrong.

"Man! My water broke. Sorry, gotta go."

In spite of himself, he had to smile. He had heard of Dinah and the coming baby. Well, Shelley would be pleased to know how that was going.

If she got her message. *If* she was ever going to answer her phone. *If* she hadn't decided that he was too old and set in his ways.

He finished his coffee. Breathed deeply. Walked a couple times around his office, giving thanks to God Almighty that Shelley was all right. Tired, but all right. Well, he knew how that was. He prayed for Dinah's baby, too. Then, with his spirit calmer and somewhat comforted, he was able to open the files on Shelley's CD, *Life After Cyrus*.

First, he saw the house. It wasn't her house or the one her father lived in now, but it was a local house. Built much like many of them in the vicinity, one-story with a tile roof, screened-in front porch, cinderblock construction. One car garage. But those were only the details he noted after he saw what had happened. A tree, with what looked to be two joined trunks, had fallen through the roof of the house. It appeared to be over the kitchen, for he could see, even through the rain in the picture, cupboards and a refrigerator. Roots were perpendicular to the ground, and Shelley herself was standing near them.

"Whoa. Shell, sweetheart, what happened?"

Stupid question. Obviously, the force of the winds for that hurricane had been enough to uproot the tree. *Whoa.*

More images followed, closer views of the destruction in the house, the rain-caused flood on the floors, the ruination of their home. Then, there was a picture with the scrawled words, "Day Two." More images. More days followed. Cleaning up. Trying to cook on a small propane stove that might have been reserved for making coffee in a campground. Stacked cans of soups. A box of frozen food that would, of course, have had to be cooked and eaten. A cooler. Blue tarps on the roof. Images of missing roofs in their neighborhood, of power cords stretched between houses, of stacks of branches as high as Shelley was tall.

He saw pictures of a rather younger Steve Sr. hanging a clothes line from a streetlight pole to a car. Pictures of twenty-year-old Shelley—her hair quite a bit longer, in a ponytail—doing laundry in a bathtub. The day marker cards went all the way to "Day Ten" before the images stopped.

He called up to Letty's desk. "Yes, Dr. Countryman?"

"Do you happen to know how strong Hurricane Cyrus was?"

"No, but Pastor will know."

"I'll ask him."

"Cat Four," was Ben's answer. "Why?"

"Shelley gave me some pictures of what happened to her and her dad when Cyrus hit, and I didn't know how strong a storm it had been."

Ben's tone was wry. "Strong. Strong enough to rip trees out of the ground and tear down signs all over town, Mark. A Category Four is about, um, let me check. Yes. Cyrus had winds maxing out at one hundred and fifty miles an hour. This latest one, Bianca, is only a Cat One right now, at eighty-five, but—"

"What?" Blinking, Mark shook his head and stared, all but unseeing, at the plaque on his wall that Shelley had made for him. "That new one is a hurricane now?"

Ben chuckled wryly. "Yeah. She was upgraded after she bounced off Cuba. We'll keep an eye on it, but if it stays close to the center of the projected path, we'll probably close up the office tomorrow."

"Thanks, Ben."

"You okay?"

"Yeah. Thanks."

He tried Shelley's phone. Again. All morning. To apologize, of course, but also to make sure she was all right. She would have been surprised—and relieved, he would guess—to know that he kept the National Hurricane Center's website and tracking page open on his computer for the rest of the day. That cone of uncertainty that the meteorologists spoke of was slowly narrowing.

Shelley finished with her calls at an hour when the office was still open. A real rarity during the winter, when she was much busier, but not so rare during the slower summer months. She wasn't contemplating the effect on her paycheck nearly as much as she was wondering what she was going to do with herself, now that she was finished with the necessary occupation of work.

"Where's Dinah?" The very-pregnant woman had opted to work until the very last minute instead of leaving on her scheduled maternity leave. Just in case she wound up being late, was what she had told Shelley. Her desk was empty now, but not at all organized. "Wait, did she—"

Ronnie, the supervisor, emerged from her office near The Empty. "Shelley, hi. Yes, Dinah went into labor this morning. Finally!"

In spite of her own stresses and preoccupations, Shelley had to smile. "Good. I'm glad. I can't imagine having to wait for something like that would be easy."

Ronnie shook her hair so that russet tresses swept over her shoulders. She looked like a model, Shelley had always thought. Happily married with two teenage boys, it didn't seem fair that she would still look so good. "It's not. Believe me. So, your dad is on vacation?"

"Yep."

"He'll miss out on the storm then. Good."

Attention sharpened, Shelley looked past Ronnie and into the supervisor's office. "How is it?"

"Cat One. Projected landfall is anywhere from Punta Gorda to Marco, right now."

"Cyrus to Willow?" Shelley said, referencing two major hurricanes that had hit their coast in her memory.

Ronnie nodded, her expression grim. "So. Keep your phone close, okay? And keep it charged. If Bianca does do either of those, we'll probably go ahead and call it a day tomorrow. I'll call you."

"And if she stalls out there?"

"We might start out here, but honestly if she's still projected anywhere near here, I know y'all will have to make preparation."

Shelley snorted in agreement. "For all these evacuation routes they have posted, it's impossible to get out of South Florida in the event of an actual emergency."

"Ain't that the truth?"

Shelley clocked out, after wishing everyone a safe day the following day. One of the girls was even planning a hurricane party. Silly. "Want to come?" she called to Shelley.

"No thanks," Shelley called on her way out. "I'll just stay home." Once in her Mini and on the way home, she started fretting. Worrying. She kept seeing Mark's face. All day. Missed talking to him. Maybe he had called; she didn't know. Her phone was home, charging.

Besides . . .

"I don't think I could have handled trying to talk to him today." No. She had had to fix patio furniture, repair an armoire that had an undocumented manufacturer's defect, repair a binding for a sofa, and install new cushion cores in a sectional. Six large cores, one small elevator. Up and down to the nineteenth floor. Her shoulders ached from the monotonous movements. But all of that was only a distraction. All she had wanted to do was call Mark and make sure he knew about the coming storm. "Stubborn, stubborn man!" she complained, pounding her steering wheel. It was about the time his office day was done. Any other Tuesday, she would be hearing from him.

"I know, I know," she answered her troublesome conscience. "I will. I'll call him. I will. It's stupid to stand on ceremony. It is. There's a hurricane on the way and the man is probably totally oblivious." Had he at least looked at the pictorial diary she and Dad had made? Did he have any clue?

She rubbed at her hair in impatience. "I'll call. I'll call. Fine. I will. I can be the bigger person. It's one stupid fight. It's not going to end the entire relationship. At least, I hope not. Ha." She all but choked, thinking it out. "We could have this entire future where we just don't speak to each other before hurricanes. Ha." Quick visuals accompanied this and she had to smile wryly at them as she crossed the Caloosahatchee Bridge. Out west. Down south. Somewhere out there, Hurricane Bianca was churning. Shelley was ready, but was *he*? Had he heard one thing? Or was he being obstinate even now?

He was in her driveway.

Her heart lurched in her chest. He wasn't supposed to be there. She couldn't breathe as she pulled into the driveway behind his Toyota. He had already climbed out, stretched to his full height, and wasn't even giving her a minute to compose herself before he approached.

He was opening her car door. "Mark," she managed, whatever she had been going to say to him on the phone—if she had been able to call him—lost as he practically pulled her out of her car and against his chest.

"Shh." Gone was the irritated and angry man from the afternoon before. *This* Mark she knew and understood. "I am so sorry," he murmured into her hair. "I really am. I don't know what—"

She wouldn't let him shoulder all of the blame. "I was a nag. I know. I'm sorry, too."

He leaned back to study her face in the light streaming from the west. "Maybe. But sweetheart, I shouldn't have disparaged your efforts. I—I didn't know what you had gone through, before, until I saw those pictures. I know it couldn't have been as—as amusing as you and your dad made it out to be for the camera."

Blushing, she leaned forward to hide her face against his throat. "At least you looked at them. Thank you."

"Are you all right?" he demanded next.

"Can't we go inside?"

"Are. You. All. Right?"

Shelley sighed heavily and pushed away from him. "I am."

His frown was heavy as she shut the door to her car. "Then where were you? I tried calling—Did you shut off your phone?—and I came here and . . . I was really worried."

She had a suspicion, based upon the tone of his voice, and gave him her driest look. "You checked to see if I was in an accident or something, didn't you?" His pained expression took her amusement away. Instead, she bracketed his face with her palms. "Mark . . . I was at my dad's. I—had to just be busy, you know? I'm sorry if I upset you. I never figured you'd think anything else."

"So, am I forgiven for being an insensitive jerk?" he asked her, his voice dark and earnest. "Honestly, Shell. I cannot believe I said those things to you." His forehead furrowed, drawing his straight brows almost into one line. "I didn't even stop to think," he went on, sounding frustrated again at his shortcomings.

She smiled and rolled up to kiss him lightly on the cheek. "Of course. Always." The tension she had been carrying around with her on calls all day loosened, so that she felt almost giddy in comparison. She wound her arms around his shoulders and was happy just looking at him. Glad that the most recent memory she had of him was now a *good* one. One in which his face was relaxed and there was *that* smile slowly surfacing.

"Oh, you need to put that one away," she murmured, half to herself.

"What?" His murmur barely helped, the devastating dimple was still there.

She blinked. "Um, nothing."

"All right then . . ." he said slowly, his eyes dancing. "So, are you going to invite me in, or do I have to finish this conversation out here in front of the neighborhood?"

"More? Finish? What?"

He laughed, throwing back his head and reaching up to grab her hands and bring them to be clasped between his own, in the space between his chest and hers. "Oh, I know it's only been thirty hours, but I have missed you."

"You counted the hours?"

He nodded, seeming a little whimsical around the edges as he kissed both her hands. "I did. So can we go in now?" He tugged her firmly toward the front door of her house. "I like the shutters. Must have been a lot of work, but they look good."

"Thanks." *Bianca!* The name of the coming storm crashed in on her awareness. "I got my dad's done, too."

Before she unlocked her door, he looked at her hands. "You're still very brave," he said, for no apparent reason that she could see.

No, I'm not, she answered silently. *Not really.*

Once indoors, curiosity about how he wanted to finish this discussion alternated with her wish to check on the storm's progress. Would it come here? Would it dance in the Gulf of Mexico for a few days and surprise everyone by going elsewhere? Would it lose its energy and peter out in the middle of the water?

But then the front door closed and suddenly, Bianca didn't matter. Not right now.

"I have something else to apologize for," Mark told her, seeming to watch her with his whole body as she emptied her pockets of her work phone, camera, keys and wallet. "And I don't know how to say so."

Her heart thumped again, hard, as if it had skipped over something. Extending her hand, she offered him her best smile. "I can't imagine what it could be," she said lightly, wanting him to know she had nothing to hold against him.

He linked his fingers with her own and led her to the sofa. She couldn't see his face for a moment or two, but what she could see had her all but dying of curiosity. The lift of his facial muscles, the strangely thoughtful turn of his lips when she could see them again. The light in his eyes—dark, but glowing all the same. She felt an answering glow burn through her own skin.

"What is it?" she whispered as he brought her down to sit beside him.

He moved a little, shifting so that he could see her face to face instead of the two of them talking to the television screen and catching each other courtesy of peripheral vision. "Sometimes," he began slowly, as if weighing his words on his tongue, "I overthink things."

She waited, nodding once. When he didn't follow that up immediately, she said, "I know. But I figured you pretty much always come up with the right answer, when you do answer. You know," she added with a saucy lift of a brow, "eventually."

"Well. I try," he murmured. "Thank you. But sometimes, it means that I—

I find excuses for myself. As if I am not responsible for acting upon what I know, if I don't know it all."

"And you're a *theologian*?" she said, still smiling.

"I'm not, no. I'm just—just a man who's trying, Shelley. Trying to teach people."

"You're an excellent teacher, you know."

He shrugged that off. "Thank you. Here I go." Shaking his head, he offered her a wan smile. "I'm doing it again. All right. This is the thing. I'm a coward."

"No. You're not." He appeared prepared to disagree, so she spoke again. "You're stubborn. You're particular about some things. You won't even *try* eggplant parmesan, but you're not a coward."

"I love you."

Her jaw dropped. She just stared at him. *No, he didn't just say that, did he?* "But I thought . . . I mean, I'm—and you're—and . . ." The words wouldn't come.

"You're not going into panic-mode, are you?" he wondered, his expression careful all of a sudden. "I didn't mean to upset you."

"Upset me?" Upset? When her brain left her body, her heart was trying to follow and her lungs had stopped breathing and . . . One coherent thought flew through her empty head and she grabbed it. "You're not apologizing for *that*, are you?"

"No," he assured her, moving his hands slowly up her arms, over the industrial grade knit shirt, until he could caress her face with his thumbs, cradling her head in very tender hands. "I'm apologizing, sweetheart, because I wish I could have told you months ago."

"Muh- Months?"

He nodded, looking regretful. "Months."

"But I thought—I thought you thought I was too young or something," she managed to say over a persistent obstruction in her throat.

"That had absolutely no bearing on how I felt for you. How I *feel* for you. It did, though, make me—make me *careful*."

She slid her hands over his arms too, turning to run her nose against his collarbone, to inhale deeply of the scent of his skin. "So, are you still being careful?" she wondered, suddenly shy. He kissed her then. Not carefully at all.

Seventeen

"If he loves you, you'll know."

"Those shutters really do make it like a cave in here," Mark observed a while later.

Shelley blinked and flicked her tongue out over kiss-swollen lips. *Mark as caveman. Yum.* Then she repeated his words to herself and steeled her resolve. "Bianca," she murmured, feeling guilty but also needing to know what was going on. "Oh, I love you, Mark. I really do, but I want to check —"

Mark blinked. "What?"

"Bianca?"

"No, I meant . . . You . . ."

Embarrassed, she sought refuge against his throat. "Sorry. Yes. I've been saying it in my head for so long myself that it just sort of slipped out." Biting her lip, she leaned back and met his incredulous expression. "I love you. You told me I was brave once, but I'm not. I just didn't want you to think I was some silly girl who said 'I love you' to every man she caught in a Gravity Well or anything," she rambled. "So I didn't, but I do."

"You love me?"

She paused a moment. "Is that all right?"

"You amaze me," he stated unequivocally. "Every single time I'm with you."

She had to smile. "I also irritate you."

"Well, only very, very rarely," he admitted, raking his hands through her hair. Then he kissed her again. Fast and hard. "And yes, of course it's all right," he whispered against her skin. Before she could react, he reached across her body for the remote control. "Here. I know you want to check. The next update isn't until eight o'clock, so if you're wanting to, oh, maybe get something to eat, we've got time."

An Unexpected Woman

Surprise held her absolutely silent for about thirty seconds, the remote control in her lap. "You—you've been watching the Weather Channel?"

"No."

Her face fell. She knew it did. It was a stupid expression maybe, but she had read it in books and now she knew exactly how it felt. "Oh."

He had a small smile in his eyes when he cupped her chin in his hand. "Oh. But I *have* had the National Hurricane Center's website open on my computer all day, so I could check for updates. Before I left to come here, I caught the Hurricane Watch color painted all over this coastline." His expression was rueful. "I also checked, and I can't think of a way to get out of here before it gets worse."

"You checked the website?" In spite of the circumstances, Shelley was quite happy. Then she got practical. "I guess it's too much to hope that you spent any part of your day checking for storm supplies, right?"

"Yes, but," he told her, standing and drawing her to her feet, "I did get a notice from the property managers at my place and they informed all of us that we have storm windows. They can't do anything about potential flooding, but I do have storm windows."

"Well," she murmured, winding her arms around his torso and giving consideration to finding sandbags, "that's something, anyway."

"So, would you like some dinner?" he asked again.

She made a quick personal inventory. "Um, I could really use a shower before we go anywhere, if that's all right."

A light sparked in his eyes. "I'll go pick us up something then, if that works for you. Let you catch up with Bianca," he went on with a warm smile, "and whatever else you feel is necessary."

"Thanks!"

When he left, Shelley took a moment to dance around her living room and down the hall, all by herself. *Oh, God, that is so extremely excellent. Thank you, thank you, thank you. And thank you that he came here and that he was worried and that he's even feeding me. Yes, I would much rather have him out getting me dinner while I'm in the shower. Yes. Definitely. I'd probably cut myself shaving, I'd be so nervous. Thank you for taking care of even these little details.*

Once actually in her bathroom, the aluminum shutter reminded her of Bianca's possible arrival in the next thirty to forty hours. Her euphoria over things being renewed with Mark was still present, but she was also thinking of what else she needed to be doing.

Well, if we're in a Cat One, it's not that big a deal, she thought, the motions of showering and shampooing automatic. *Cat Two, same thing, but I'll be glad to have the shutters. Too much stronger, and we can always go in the closet.*

Her closet, the one in the master bedroom, she had retrofit into a hurricane-reinforced room. Not wanting to feel as vulnerable as she had during Cyrus, not ever again, she and Dad and Stephanie had spent time reinforcing the walls and the ceiling over her closet, enlarging it by about three feet on two of the sides, so that she could put in a proper storm door with a lock. Steel plates, anchor bolts, and hurricane straps had been installed in their proper places and she felt very good about it all. Plus, she had a bigger closet than she had ever had in her life.

She raided that closet now, selecting a red top—as he had stated that red was a favorite color—and a pair of shorts. "Mark?" she called in some trepidation out her bedroom door. "Back yet?"

No answer. Good. Fluffing her hair out with her fingers, she returned to the living room and turned the television back to the Weather Channel.

Mark came back with Chinese, and took two of the square, metal-handled boxes to her refrigerator. "For tomorrow," was all he said, his voice coming from the kitchen. "Just in case we need a little extra."

"We?" Shelley asked, setting their food out on her table.

Since this had become something of a regular thing for them to do, Mark knew where everything was in the kitchen, and he emerged with glasses and soda. His expression was smooth. "We. If you think, Miss Roberts, that I am not going to keep an eye on you during a hurricane, you have another think coming, as my dad always says."

"Well, Pastor Mark, then I guess you should bring over whatever meager supplies you did manage to stash away when you come back tomorrow."

His phone rang just as his chopsticks were halfway to his mouth, chow mein noodles dripping dangerously. "My sister."

By the time his family had all managed to call him, his dinner was cold and she was reheating it for him. He finished eating and she camped in front of the television so she was able, when it came, to tell him about the latest information from the National Hurricane Center.

"Mark."

"What?"

"She's a Category Two now."

"Let's pray," he suggested immediately. Joining her on the living room floor, he took her hands in his, blew out a concerned breath, and bowed his head.

Some time later they agreed to keep in touch the next day, regarding their different schedules. "Sure it'll be all right if you're here?" she asked him, cocking her head and wondering. "I mean, a hurricane doesn't just come and go like a movie or something. You could be stuck here all night."

"Really?"

"Yep."

"They last that long?"

"Well, if the power does go out, we'll be set on a curfew, because the traffic lights'll be out. At least, that's happened before. It's not safe to drive in the dark when it's like that. Though," she went on, remembering, "some media people might be out and about. But they're exceptions."

"You said I'm in a flood zone, right?"

"You are. Category One. I have a hurricane closet if it gets too bad."

He shook his head, a knowing smile lifting his lips. "Why am I not surprised?"

He left for home early, in order to do what he could to ready his own place in case the storm blew up the river the following day. She admonished him to charge his cell phone all night, and any laptop batteries. "You never know. Might be no reason for it, but—"

"Better to be safe than sorry. I know."

At the door, he cupped her face in his hands. "Stay here tonight, all right? I almost went crazy wondering where you were last night."

"I'm so sorry. I really am." And tonight, she was, though last night she hadn't considered how he felt, only how *she* had felt. That had been selfish. "I'll behave, honest."

"I love you," he whispered before kissing her good night. "And I cannot tell you what a relief it is to actually say it."

"I think I have some idea," she informed him. He only gave her that dangerous, dimpled smile before leaving her for the night.

She thought it might be silly, but even so she dragged the duvet out of the guest room closet. It was really, really expensive stuff. But she had got it for a song, because it had been special-ordered for a customer who had then changed his mind. The warehouse's clearance sales were seriously good for people who were flexible and had some skill with upholstery. Duvet on the floor like a mattress, pillow and sheet, Shelley bedded down in front of the television that night to keep an eye on the weather. But though the Hurricane Watch changed to a Hurricane Warning, meaning that everyone had best make final preparations "to protect life and property," the smile still lingered in her eyes.

He loves me.

There was a song out by the group Casting Crowns, called "I Praise You in This Storm". The lyrics, as sung by the group, echoed in Mark's mind most of the night. Part of it, he knew, was simply the idea that a storm was coming. He had awakened a couple of times, his mind obviously on edge, and had seen Bianca's projected path look more and more like the storm would be greeting Southwest Florida pretty much on his lanai.

That didn't bother him, though. What he had here was just stuff. Nice stuff, but *stuff*. He was expecting to take some precious, irreplaceable items, and the "meager supplies" he had to Shelley's house. The rest was replaceable.

The most important thing was Shelley herself. Her laughter. Her spirit.

She loved him. He had been surprised, mostly because he had so misunderstood what she had been offering him. He did not feel any check in his spirit about her, so could only suppose that whatever it had been that had troubled him before was not an issue.

Which was good. *Today has enough worries of its own.*

Ben Keller called shortly before eight. "We're canceling everything tonight, Mark. We should be far enough inland not to have any real flooding problems, but if you have the opportunity and can come, I'd appreciate your help here."

"Of course. I'll be right there. Do you need a set of hands for power tools or anything?"

Ben's laugh was lined with exhaustion. "Oh, sure. If she's not too busy. Doesn't she have preparations to make herself?"

"Shelley? You would not believe the fortress she has ready and waiting."

"For a Category Two?"

"Better to be safe . . ." Mark let the rest of the proverb go without saying.

The rest of the morning, and on past lunch, went by in a blur. Shelley drove to her dad's house for his tools, and worked alongside some of the younger men, lifting, balancing, hammering, and even laughing and cracking jokes. She was so much more at her ease doing this than talking about crochet or children with the women of the church. It made perfect sense to him. She would say she had prepared for this, naturally.

His own brushings with jealousy, he set aside. She was who she was, and she talked to everyone in just that same playful, encouraging tone. It had captivated him months ago. Maybe even the very first time she had touched him.

She must have felt him watching her for a few moments, because she found his eyes across the green lawn and smiled, lifting a two-by-four in one arm and some sort of power tool in the other. "You're something else," he murmured.

They were just finishing up and putting tools away, as well as making sure all the playground equipment was secure and any loose chairs, benches, and other light equipment had been stowed somewhere safe, when the rains started coming. Mark looked up at the word "rainbands" being tossed about by those who had lived here long enough to have been through a hurricane season or two. Those clouds, moving rapidly high above, seemed to be sculpted. Rain poured down for minutes at a time before moving on.

The winds started growing stronger, causing the palm trees to bend. Sometimes with grace, sometimes abruptly, but bend they did, their green fronds seeming to stretch out like multiple arms away from the wind.

"Time to go," Shelley called, pushing spikes of short brown hair from her forehead. "Stuff's going to start blowing around pretty soon."

Just as they were leaving the church—she with a power screwdriver in one hand and a tool belt around her waist—a dark sedan with a rental sticker from a local company drove around the sheltered drop-off point by the front door. A man got out, looking rushed, interested, and distracted. His dark hair and salt and pepper beard reminded Mark of nothing so much as someone who might be in public relations.

"Can I help you?" he called, since he was the nearest staff member available.

From out of his black leather jacket, the newcomer withdrew a card. "Hi. Kevin McGrew, from Vancouver. Got here because my magazine is doing a story on North American weather for a big spread later this year, and this hurricane seemed to be perfectly timed. Been driving around looking for something public I could check on. You guys seem to be it. So—" he went on, moving with alacrity to the trunk of the car, "let me get my camera and tripod out, if that's all right with you?"

Mark felt that this Kevin McGrew had all the force of nature, and he was pleased enough to nod his permission.

"Great! I can't thank you enough." He took out a camera with what seemed to be an enormous lens, and then promptly covered it in something that looked like a red nylon sock. The logo said it was a Storm Jacket. That, Mark thought, made a whole lot of sense. McGrew smiled easily, in spite of his apparent need for speed. "I know you have to get going, so let me just ask you a few things before you do." He clicked on a tiny recorder about the size of a pen, and asked what seemed to Mark to be a pre-planned set of questions while he gauged distances and light conditions.

Only Shelley Roberts, Mark guessed, would be able to give a fully coherent interview about hurricanes when one was beating on her head. McGrew asked her for a few cogent details before a stronger gust of wind surprised him.

"Let me get your phone numbers, if that's all right. I'll be in touch," the photojournalist told them, walking rapidly away from them to take a quick survey of the church buildings. "I've got to get some shots now, before this wind gets worse."

"We'll look forward to hearing from you, won't we, Mark?" Shelley said as McGrew checked his lens and focus and did something to some buttons on his camera.

"Of course." Then to Shelley, he whispered, "Come on. I'd like to get back to your fortress before this gets much worse."

Her laugh was indignant. "My fortress?"

"That's what I'm calling it." She rolled her eyes at him, but didn't dispute it further.

"I think," she said as they pulled away from the church, leaving Ben to the tender mercies of the Canadian photojournalist, "that I'll keep Dad's tools with me. Just in case."

"What happened to yours?"

"His are—were—fresher. I'll recharge everything. At least, I will if we get to keep the power on."

She was in the house while he was still opening the trunk of his car. "I have to see how strong this thing is," she called back. Mark nodded and started getting what he had brought out of the trunk of his car. Shelley would help when her need to know had been satisfied.

She did reappear, biting her lip but not saying anything as she hefted the flat of bottled water he had brought. She tossed the batteries on top of it and then lost her preoccupied expression as her eyes lit on a framed portrait still in the trunk of his car.

"Oh, Mark. Who're they?"

"My grandparents," he replied with a fond smile, the memories swimming with pleasant associations. "They passed away when I was in college. I brought some pictures and other things," he warned her, meeting her eyes over the stack of things in her arms and the bundles in his own. "I hope it's all right."

"Of course. I have a spare room, you know. We can put all of your things in there."

A change of clothes, toiletries, the pictures. So few things really, but it did, for a brief moment, feel very strange to be bringing his personal items into Shelley's house. The need for it was real. No one could fault him for safeguarding such things, nor for wanting to be with her when there was danger literally in the air. Still . . . it felt a little strange. The meerkats, bless their hearts, would likely take exception, if and when this became more generally known.

Once his car was secure and her doors were locked, Shelley met his eyes across the living room, with a new team of meteorologists sharing the latest updates behind her on the television.

"Well?" Mark asked, rocking up on the toes of his sneakers. "Anything else we need to do?"

"Wait," she said with a small smile and a shrug. "And pray."

And then, there was an ominous series of musical notes from the Weather Channel. "Bianca has strengthened since our last update," the female half of the new team said, her voice devoid of any regional accent. "The latest readings show that Bianca's sustained winds are now holding at one hundred and thirty-five miles per hour."

Shelley turned slowly to face the wide screen, her mouth open. "Cyrus," she whispered.

"As Hurricane Cyrus surprised everyone living in Southwest Florida," the male meteorologist elaborated, his voice smooth but urgent, "Bianca has stunned the National Weather Service and shattered predictions by such rapid intensification. The unseasonably warm waters of the Gulf of Mexico are undoubtedly a large contributor to this change."

"Fortunately," the woman said, taking over in front of a map, "you can see by this satellite imagery that Bianca—like Cyrus—is also a small, fast-moving storm. If you're in the Punta Gorda, Fort Myers or Naples regions, you should do what you can to make sure you are as safe as possible from such strong winds."

Mark didn't recall crossing the room to wrap Shelley up against his chest.

He only knew that, as the sky suddenly darkened outside the clear shutters that she had on her street-side windows, he was holding her to himself, willing his heart to slow down. *Lord God. Please, watch over us and over everyone.* His thoughts flew to the church and those who were part of his life there, too. And then, to the photographer from Canada. And to the neighborhood. He could see the images from Shelley's digital album from several years before, and closed his eyes briefly. Faith, he had trusted in for years. Faith, as was taught in the book of James. *Faith. Preparation*, Shelley had insisted.

They would need both.

"So," Mark said after a few moments, "you said you had a hurricane closet?"

Eighteen
"It's a gift from God himself."

"I do, but it's full!" Shelley's mind was racing, thinking of what had happened last time. "You know," she said, her voice too calm to be real, "I remember you asking me something about the odds."

Behind her, Mark's arms tightened as he kissed the top of her head. "I'm sorry. Yeah. Odds don't work with the weather." She heard him sigh. "Well, you said you had a closet, right? We don't have to go in there until it's a lot worse though, I'm guessing. I can't imagine sitting in a closet for the next several hours."

The image distracted Shelley long enough to turn in his arms and smile up at him with a teasing air. "No?" She playfully batted her lashes, wanting to sidetrack him. "We'll have to work on your imagination then, Mark." She was delighted that she had distracted him enough to bring color to his face.

"Why don't you help me?" he suggested. "Give me a frame of reference?" With a smile, he nuzzled the skin at her temple.

But she was thinking he was absolutely right. "Of course. And, we can get it ready so we don't have to freak out about it later." Kissing him quickly, she wriggled from his embrace and took off down the hall. "Well? Come on." Oh, she could guess what kind of reference he was hinting at, but she knew that it was going to be *interesting enough* for the next several hours with him and so much . . . What was it her mom had called it? *Zing?* Yes, that. *Zing* in the house. And no other outlet, really. Much better to find something else to do.

She knew that he knew it too, and he would respect her decision. Mark did the right thing, and he did it the right way. *Well, almost always.*

Which was why she had no qualms about having him in her bedroom or in her closet. None at all. "I've been in here before," he told her, surprising

An Unexpected Woman

her so that she halted in mid-step.

"You have?"

"The night you were injured, remember? I came in here for a blanket for you." His expression was loving, but with an edge of regret that she had been hurt that day. "Didn't peek, I promise."

"Of course you didn't. You're an honorable guy!"

He studied her for a moment. "Thank you." She leaned against the wall as he remained poised in the doorframe. "So. What frame of reference were *you* thinking of giving me?" he asked, with a slight emphasis that made her smile as she turned from him to go to the closet.

"The closet. Can you help?" She opened the door. "If you could take these things, here," she said, pointing at her hangers of clothes, "then I can get the emergency stuff and put it inside so we have some supplies . . ." Playfulness dropped from her. "Supplies. Just in case."

"Of course. But Shelley," he went on, making no immediate move to step through the closet door to get her clothing, "have some faith too, all right? You've done *everything* humanly possible. The rest of it is up to God."

She blushed. He was right. She couldn't control everything. "Sorry," she said on a sigh. "I'll do better when—when we're ready."

Expecting his disbelieving laughter, she was not surprised when it came. "All right then. Where do you want me to put all of these, um," he gestured vaguely at her skirts and tops and dresses. "These?"

"The guest room—no," she said, immediately blushing again. "Um. The work room. Remember it? Where the computer is?" *Where we had our fight?* she did not add.

He remembered. Nodded as if he did, anyway. "Got it. All right."

Leaving him to it, she cleared out of the closet. What did she need? Storm radio. Just in case. Right. Batteries. The battery-powered lantern. Munchies. She had some freeze-dried fruit snacks from Costco. Bottled water. Oh, the duvet for the floor. If they did have to sit in there, another layer of padding would be nice. Pillows, too. Good.

Gathering all of these things, she deposited them on the middle of her bed and ran back to the television. Just to see if Bianca had changed her mind.

Mark finished hanging up all of Shelley's clothes from her closet. Then, something struck him so that he stepped back and saw the pattern. A definitive pattern. Right in front of his eyes. It floored him completely, so that he fell back against the wall behind him in subdued shock.

Ribbons and bows. On almost everything she owned.

"Oh, Lord," he whispered as incredulous amazement coursed through his whole body. "Really? Is *this* what I've been *missing*?" Sheer delight.

Still staring, open-mouthed, at the clothing now hanging in her workroom closet, he was overwhelmed. *I know I said I didn't deserve her. But you didn't mean me to, did you? She has always been a gift. A gift. You, my Lord, blow me away. Thank you.* A new sort of surety settled solidly within him. Oh, he loved her, he wanted to ask her to be his wife, but this—

"Mark? Are you back here? Was there too much stuff? I can make room if you need—" Her sudden stop just inside the doorway was accented by an expression of intense curiosity. "What? What is it?"

He didn't know what to say, so he held his arm out to her. She came to him and he wrapped her up against himself, still brimming over with thanksgiving. "I love you," he murmured again. "And I finally figured out what was bothering me."

"I love you too, and I'm so glad, but what is it?" She tilted her head back, and he relished just the opportunity of watching her eyes as her emotions flew behind them. Emotions, questions, all the things that made her who she was.

After brushing his lips across her forehead, he told her. "I told you I overthink things."

"Yes."

"That's what it was. Well that, and that I completely did not see what God had given me."

Her smile was crooked. "And what was that?"

"You."

"Me?"

"I asked, a long time ago, for the Lord to—well, to keep me from making any more mistakes. In relationships. You know?"

"I knew you had stories in there somewhere," she murmured. He was just thankful she didn't press for them right now.

He nodded, inhaling the fresh scent of her shampoo. "And I asked him—don't laugh—I asked him to let me know when he was sending me the right woman."

"How?" she wondered.

He closed his eyes, then opened them to turn her around and look at the closet. "I asked him to gift wrap her for me. With a bow."

He felt the snap of surprise that shot through her. "Are you kidding me? You asked *God* that? *Seriously*?" She turned and stared at him. "Wow."

"Wow, indeed. And then, first time I see you out of uniform, there you are, with that knock-out dress and I didn't even notice. And I'm standing here now, thinking I must be the blindest man in America not to have seen it. You have nothing *but* ribbons and bows in there. And I completely didn't get it."

"So I'm a present?" she asked, laughter sparkling in her voice. "Oh, my."

He refused to overthink it again. "Come on."

"We've got this big storm outside, Mark."

"I know, come on. Just to the kitchen."

"You're *hungry*? Right *now*?"

His heart was rejoicing so that even Bianca couldn't dampen his purpose. "No. But come on. I left something for you."

"In my *kitchen*?"

He had her hand in his, so he pulled her to one side as he opened the fridge. "In here," he instructed, pointing to the box set farther back on the shelf.

She took the box from China Town, its metal handle cold. "Lunch?"

"Open it."

Something of his anticipation undoubtedly communicated itself to her, as the winds picked up to whistle around the aluminum shutters outside her window. The rain sounded like rocks being thrown at the house. Still, all this was peripheral. His concentration was focused on Shelley's face.

"Mark?" He didn't say anything, so she undid the little combination of flaps and slots that would open the box. Her eyes grew huge when the small white box was open entirely and she could see what was inside. "Oh, Mark."

He retrieved the box from her suddenly trembling hands, touched and maybe trembling himself. "I think," he said, surprised at how rough his voice sounded. "I think." He cleared his throat to try again. "I think that I can't remember what I wanted to say to you."

She laughed a little, but it sounded choked. Her eyes were filling, right in front of him. "I haven't a clue," she whispered.

He withdrew the diamond solitaire he had purchased the night before, set the box aside, and took her left hand in his, concentrating. "Then I'll just ask. Will you marry me?"

"Do you even have to ask? Wasn't I gift wrapped and dropped in front of you? Special delivery from, like, Heaven-Express or something?"

Her breathless laughter relaxed him so that he was able to meet her incandescent eyes. "Actually, I think *I* was dropped right in front of *you*."

"You were," she said on a breath, obviously remembering their very first meeting. "Oh, wow. Oh, Mark, this is so absolutely perfect. Absolutely."

"Is that a yes?"

"Yes! Yes! Of course! Yes!"

She was laughing, crying, and trying to wrap herself around him in the next heartbeat. He held her close, amazed and still feeling steeped in wonder. Even when, in the next minute, there was a huge crack of electricity from somewhere and the house was plunged into darkness.

"Well."

Heart still racing with the wonder of Mark's proposal, Shelley had to wrench her mind from him, tear her body from his, and address both the darkness and Mark's one-word statement. The word and its tone told her better than anything else that he trusted that she had made provision for this exact happening.

The power outage, not the marriage proposal.

"The shutters are clear in the living room," she reminded him. "So you should be able to see your way there in a moment."

"Ah, yes, so why are you rummaging in that drawer next to me?"

The sound was unmistakable. She grinned. "Flashlight."

"If there's light," he inquired, his voice almost comically reasonable, "why do you need a flashlight?"

"How hot are Julys in South Florida, honey?" she asked with a ton of sugar in her voice. "Do you hear the air conditioner?"

"Ah. No. So you have—"

"Battery powered fans for now. A generator for later."

There was a faint hint of grayish light that filtered tepidly around the corner of the kitchen from the living room. In it, she saw the dark pools where Mark's eyes were, and she traced the outline of his face. He smiled under her fingertips. "Of course. Remind me to tell you how incredibly grateful I am for you."

"Later," she agreed on a breath. "Go in the living room. I'll get us some stuff."

Before too long, they were in the living room with her storm radio and a fan to keep the air moving. Just beyond Shelley's Lexan-shuttered window, Bianca raged. A storage shed rolled down the middle of the street, and even through the layers of Lexan and glass, she and Mark could hear the rough scraping sound it made on the asphalt.

The day wore on, hour by hour. She changed the batteries in the fan, but refrained from using any flashlights just yet. Suddenly, Mark—who was at the window—gasped. "Oh, God, no."

Before she knew what he was doing, he had unlocked her front door and taken off at a run. And then she could see why. Across the street, a huge cypress tree in the front yard was uprooted and had just crashed through the roof.

"Cyrus," she whispered, momentarily welded to the spot as Mark took off, his path uneven as he had to resist the incredible winds and was pelted with the rock-hard rain.

She took off after him. "Mark, it's a vacant house. Mark!"

As soon as she left the shelter of her front porch, the full force of the hurricane hit her. As if an entire baseball team was throwing rocks at her. Her face stung, but she had to get to him.

"Mark!"

There he was, calling out, his voice audible even over the howling winds. No one would answer. He didn't know that though, and he was trying desperately to get past the tree and into the ruined bedrooms of the home.

"Mark!"

"Shelley, help me!"

She got to him, wrapped her arms around him and made him face her. She was strong enough to turn him against his will. "No, hon, no. Stop. No one's here. It's vacant. No one's here."

The sense of it got through to him, and he leaned against the wall that was standing and holding up the trunk of the tree. That trunk gave him partial shelter from Bianca's assault. He met her gaze, looking exhausted and self-conscious. "Sorry," he called. Though not much space separated them, the weather required the volume. "Guess you got bombarded, too?"

"Totally worth it," she said to assure him, summoning a smile. "Ready to do it again?" She held out her hand.

He took it and they both glanced down. Her engagement ring sparkled in the cloud-diffused light that still pervaded the sky. "I'm ready," he said with a nod.

They had taken a couple steps into the wildness beyond the tree trunk when she turned her head to keep from getting hit in the face with the punishing rain. *Oh no, what's that?* She opened her eyes further and froze, her gut a ball of ice within her.

"Shelley! Come on!"

A funnel cloud was up there. Down the street and past the last house on the end. The white one with the long driveway. It was an empty driveway, as were so many of them these days, but there it was. "Oh, no. Oh, no. Oh, no. Oh, no."

"Shelley!"

She didn't know what he did, only that she couldn't seem to think. *Tornado!* She wasn't ready for a tornado. Oh, she knew they came sometimes during or after a hurricane, but not here. She wasn't ready. No!

Squinting against the wind, Mark came to stand between her and the whirling monster that seemed to be approaching. "Shelley, come inside! To your closet. Come on!"

"Yes, of course," she murmured, allowing him to pull her. She didn't even feel the rain right then. Her whole focus was on the gray and black invader that was screaming like a train as it touched down.

Panic-mode. She wasn't thinking. Mark got over his inner embarrassment at having run to rescue an empty house in the heartbeat it took for him to understand what was happening.

Tornadoes? Why hadn't he paid closer attention to all this stuff? Castigating himself for being all kinds of an educated idiot, he led Shelley back through her front door and locked it. They were saturated. Too bad. No time to do anything about it now.

"Your closet," he repeated to her, as she stood, wide-eyed, just inside the door. "Come on, Shell. Come on." He barely had the presence of mind to latch onto one of her flashlights as they passed the end table in the living room. Down the hall to her room, it was dark, so he pushed the black rubber button on the flashlight to make sure neither of them stepped on anything as they got into her closet.

"Now what?" *Lord, help me. I'm not the one who's done this before!*

She was getting her breath back thankfully. "Um, lock the door. Keep the flashlight. I've got stuff in here." Her words were choppy, and she seemed to still be listening, as if she expected the runaway train sound they had heard to engulf her house, too.

On the floor, she had what looked like blankets or something to sit on. Pillows, yes. He sank down to them, pulling her down to join him, settling her so that he had his arms around her and could keep her warm. He needed warmth, too.

"Sweetheart? Are you all right?" He felt her heart still racing through her back to his chest. He spoke right next to her ear, trying to keep his voice calm for her. "We're as safe as we can be, Shell. You did a great job preparing."

"I didn't plan for a tornado," she confessed, sounding distraught. She leaned over to turn on a battery powered camping lantern. He shut off the flashlight. "I'm sorry. I lost it again."

"It's all right. You're fine and I'm fine and that's all that matters."

"But what if it comes here?" she whispered tightly.

"Didn't you reinforce this thing to a fare-thee-well?"

"A what?"

"You did as much as you could, Shelley. We should be fine."

"But what if we're not?"

He turned her to face him, huddled as they were at the bottom of her closet, shoes stacked on a rack to one side, and a piece of notebook paper moving on a low shelf. The paper vibrated with Shelley's every breath until he turned her to look at him. "If we're not safe? Shelley, I can't think of a better person to watch the end of the world with," he said, caressing the chilled skin on her cheeks and arms and knees.

"End of the world?" That got her to smile a little, so that she shook herself and threw off her panic-induced bewilderment. "You really are my best friend. I'm so glad," she said, leaning suddenly into him.

"All right. I have to tell you, it was kind of a blow to my ego when you kept telling me how much you were just thrilled about being friends." He kissed her wet hair. "I don't know how it was in South Carolina," he said, smiling as she looked curiously up at him in the unshaded light of the lantern, "but for me, that was never a good thing."

"Being friends?" She appeared distressed and he did not want that, so he tried again.

"As opposed to, you know, being more than friends."

"Oh. Oh, my." She pulled her lower lip between her teeth. "I won't apologize, though, because it's something my mom said to look for." She wrinkled her nose up at him.

"What?" He said that often around Shelley, but he secretly hoped that would never really change.

She turned and eyed him speculatively. He could hear no hint of a storm. The tornado must have passed on. *Thank you, Lord God Almighty, maker of Heaven and Earth. Thank you.* No light passed around the heavy, locked closet door, but at least where they were, right now, in this small space, they were safe. And Shelley was completely *here*, in her usual frame of mind. *Thank you.*

"I think I can show you." Her voice was soft now. Soft, and holding something very precious. "I think she'd be all right with that." He saw how her focus dropped briefly to the diamond he had put on her finger not long ago, and smiled to himself. "Yes. I think she would."

He took her hand in his. "Show me what?"

"Her last letter to me." She took the piece of notebook paper from the shelf that had been close to her face and gave it to him. "If there's light enough, I mean."

Fascinated, and feeling very conscious of this singular trust she was giving him—another gift—he took the paper and began to read. "Should I read it out loud?" he asked softly, not knowing how she wanted this handled, this sharing of her mother's final words.

"No." The one-word refusal was only a breath.

Gathering her against himself again, he held the letter close to the camping lantern as they sat on the floor, pillows behind his back. He read and felt Shelley's breathing change, as if she had read this letter so often she knew exactly where he was based on how long he had been reading it.

> Happy 21st Birthday, Shelley!
>
> As I write this, you're in school. Fifth grade. You haven't the faintest notion of getting married. You mostly like playing baseball with your brother, when he lets you. You have scabs on your knees, you like popping your shoulders in and out of their sockets, and find your greatest joy in jumping from the highest places you can get to. Still, I am guessing that by the time you are reading this letter, you will have more of a thought about "boys". Here are some of mine.
>
> First things first. The Lord says for his children not to be "unequally yoked" with unbelievers. If you have asked Jesus into your heart, you're a believer. And you should not "yoke" yourself with someone who is not. So I would pray for you, Shelley, that when you do start meeting men and wondering whom to marry, that this will be a priority for you. That your man will be God's man.

Secondly, do not yoke yourself to a man unless he has a sense of humor compatible with yours. In life, the ability to laugh is vital. More vital than almost anything, I think, in a marriage. So remember this, daughter. Remember to find a man that makes you laugh and who will laugh with you. Not at you. Except, maybe, when it's called for. If he loves you, you'll know.

Third, do not forget the zing! My mother told me that and now I'm telling you. It's third on my list, the feeling of sexual attraction. Chemistry. That feeling that makes your palms damp, your heart race, and your words tumble over themselves when you talk to the Special One. I remember dating your dad. Oh, the time I had! Wanting the man you want to marry—wanting him with your body and your heart and your mind—is not a sin. It's not. It's a gift from God himself.

Fourth, I would pray that the man you marry is your friend. Your dad is my best friend. My very best earthly companion. We can talk about just about everything, and we have. Find a man that is a friend, in addition to all the rest, darling daughter, and you will have found a companion for your life that will bring you joy and laughter, in good times and bad, during the whole of your marriage.

Marriage, my girl, is work. It may seem like your dad and I don't work too hard at our life together, but we do. We promised we would. So whenever God sends you that Special One he wants for you to share your life with, and things get rough around the edges or even in the middle (like that uneven gingerbread we baked on our last Christmas together), work with it.

I know that your dad will do the best he can to be both a mother and a father to you. He will. I know him like I know my own self. But someday, he might find that he's lonely again, and that he wants another companion in his life. Know this, Shelley. I want him to find someone to love again. God says that a man is not meant to live alone always. So if your dad chooses to find a new wife someday, support him. Pray for him to choose well. And welcome her. Know that I hope he will be able to laugh again with someone. I have even told him so.

And someday, Shelley, I believe we will all be together in Heaven. All of us. I can't wait!

Happy Birthday, for now and forever.

I love you!

Mom

He finished it, and didn't know what to say, aside from the quiet "Thank you" that he whispered to her. He was overwhelmed; there were no words sufficient. Her breath caught and she sniffled. The way her tense shoulders shook against him, told him that she was feeling vulnerable and sad. Hoping to offer silent comfort, he brushed his lips down the side of her throat before shutting off the lantern so she could compose herself in the darkness.

He just held her, letting his mind work through what he had just read. No wonder Shelley had been so enthusiastic about being friends. It meant that she had been thinking, all these months that they had been together, of what her mother had written. Of marriage. Of linking her life with his. *All these months . . .* He was entirely humbled. He was ten feet tall. He felt his whole spirit run over in thanksgiving to a wonderful, gifting God, who had been preparing this woman for him.

She stirred in the cradle of his arms and he felt her lips brush his jaw. "Thank you." He was about to respond when she moved a little restlessly. He heard her inhale, as if ready to start a race, before sliding from his embrace. "It sounds pretty quiet out there. I guess my house is still standing."

Very practical, his fiancée. "Shall we find out?"

"Yes, please, but first," she said, her voice rising with her body in the dark confines of the closet, "will you kiss me? I confess that I've had that on my mind since you got here today."

"Kissing you in the closet?"

Her chuckle was higher up. "Yep. I'm afraid I'm hopelessly into you, Dr. Mark Countryman."

Laughing, finding her hand in the absolute darkness of the closet, he pushed himself upright as well. "Well that's good, because the feeling is definitely mutual." He found her lips after sliding from the strong line of her jaw, tasting the storm and a bit of her sorrow on her skin before moving to her mouth. Her hands gripped his shoulders before one moved to his hair. He loved her physical strength, reveled in it, and responded by gripping her more tightly against himself. Heat flared, his heart pounding more heavily than it had when he'd run into the pelting rain. When he had to breathe, he moved only the barest inch from her face. "I love you."

She sighed, a contented sound, and he smiled in the security of her closet.

When they opened the door to the dark, warm house, the first thing Mark noticed was the relative quiet. Reaching back for the lantern, he turned it on again so that he and Shelley could navigate.

"It all looks good," she said, her voice tentative.

"Want to check outside?" He prayed that no one had been hurt, but had a morbid interest in the damage caused by the tornado.

They opened the front door to gauge the winds, and were pleased enough that Bianca's main body seemed to have blown north and east of them. He gave a fleeting thought to his condo, but knew nothing could be done about it now.

Darkness had settled as a tangible presence, without a streetlight or porch light to relieve its oppression. Frogs were the first thing he heard, aside from the comparatively gentle rain that still fell. "Wow."

"I know. Last time, I had this thought that this was what the Calusa people had to deal with, you know? The total quiet. At least 'til the generators get started."

"Yeah. So, do you want to see if anyone's out there? Make sure no one needs help?"

Shelley held back for a moment. Then, "Of course. Yes. Let me get our phones, though. Just in case."

"Do you think any of the cell towers will be working?"

"Better to have them than not," she countered from a shadowy corner.

A slow search of the storm-damaged structures on the street revealed that many of the houses with the greatest damage were vacant. The tornado had taken no lives there that day. He praised God with each empty house he saw, thinking—though Shelley would scoff—of the odds of that happening. *Thank you,* he prayed silently. *Thank you.* He saw some candles, flashlights and other lanterns as he and Shelley walked in near silence back to her house. "This is eerie," he admitted.

Unexpectedly, she stopped in front of her house at the rear bumper of his car and wrapped her arms around his shoulders. "It may be, but I also think it's romantic. This is our engagement day, and I'll remember it forever."

She never ceased to amaze him. "I adore you," he murmured just before she reached his lips with hers.

What a gift.

Epilogue

"Marriage, my girl, is work."

"Mark? I'm home!"

"Back here," he called from the workroom.

Shelley tossed her wallet, keys, work phone, personal cell phone, and camera on the dining table in their usual conglomeration of clutter and went to find him. He was at the computer—newer, nicer, now that they were married and he had an official Home Office he liked to work from on occasion. She kissed the back of his neck. "How's it going?"

He stood to wrap her up in his arms. They had spent one whole month now as husband and wife, and she looked forward to the coming moments as the best part of her day. He kissed her, but seemed preoccupied.

"Okay. How'd your day go?"

Still watching his face to see if she could get an idea about what was on his mind, Shelley shrugged a little. "Well, Dinah brought little Ethan to work today. Her babysitter was in an accident and so she had to bring the baby herself. He's doing great," she added with a fond smile. "Sat up all by himself and everything. But he got hold of my call sheet, so that was kind of a mess."

Mark chuckled and lost that preoccupied air for a moment. "I can imagine. Joanna's kids were obsessed with paper when they were babies."

His voice dropped into a heavy, contemplative place and she waited before leaning in to nuzzle his throat.

"What is it?" she wondered, her voice muffled. "Someone at church?" She knew that if it was, he couldn't talk about it and his preoccupation would be officially invisible to her.

He shook his head and moved so that he could hold her hands. "Come on."

A talk. Those sometimes unsettled her. She didn't know why, except that they tended to come without warning. They were never bad, though. Never. Just serious Moments from the Mind of Mark, as she thought of them. She loved him in all his moods, and this was just another one.

He settled himself down on the sofa and pulled her to sit across his lap, her legs stretched out on the cushions while his were on the coffee table. "I got an e-mail today."

"Oh? From who?"

"Lily Mitchell, from Athens, Ohio." He eyed her as if she would know who this was.

She had to think. A face did filter through, though, eventually. One of the meerkats. She blushed. "Oh? And how is she?"

"Doing well. Thing is this: She's on the pastoral search committee for her church up there. You know she's only here as an Associate Member, right?"

Shelley nodded, intent upon the minute shifting of his expressions as he explained. "The whole snowbird thing. I know. And?"

He took her hand in his so that he could slide his fingers in and out of hers, brushing against her wedding ring over and again. She smiled and sank against the pillows that were fluffed against the arm of the sofa. He stopped and offered her a strange little smile. "Well. It seems that she has nominated me to be their new Senior Pastor, up there at her church. We are invited to stay with them for a week. I'll have to nail down dates with you and with the church."

"The church in Athens?"

He nodded, studying her face. "Yes."

"So what's the problem? Senior Pastor, Mark? That'd be excellent!" Then she frowned a little. "I could never be Annie Keller though."

He laughed and bent to brush his lips over her forehead. "You make a much better Shelley Countryman."

"Too true." Still, she frowned and wondered how she would really go over in Ohio.

"Sweetheart, Lily Mitchell knows you and likes you. *And* your power tools *and* your crocheting needles."

She blew out a slow breath. "So . . . What do we do next?"

"Well, I wanted you to know what was going on. Because there are no hurricanes or tropical storms in Athens, you know. I used to work near there. In Parkersburg."

She rolled her eyes at him. "I think I can live without hurricanes, hon. So what do they have in Athens, Ohio?"

"Occasional blizzards?"

Eyes alight, she launched herself from his lap to run down the hall.

"Where are you going?" Mark called after her, missing the weight of her body already, and thinking about all the work she had put into this house of hers. Of theirs. Had he sent her into another one of her panic modes?

"I'm in the office. Checking out blizzard preparations."

On the sofa, Mark laughed to himself and shook his head. Well, he knew how to handle that, too.

"Of course you are," he remarked mildly. He took a much slower trip back to the office, caught her eye and started unbuttoning his shirt. She watched, eyes widely focused on his chest, fingers frozen over the keyboard in front of her. He suppressed his smile, but turned to go to their room a few steps away. "I'll be waiting for you when you're done."

The End

CPSIA information can be obtained at www.ICGtesting.com
Printed in the USA
LVOW01s0522091013

356113LV00001B/7/P